Black

A NOVEL BY F. G. PACI

Madonna

ISBN 0 88750 419 1 (hardcover)
ISBN 0 88750 420 5 (softcover)

Book design by Michael Macklem

Printed in Canada

PUBLISHED IN CANADA BY OBERON PRESS

For Christine

1

Joey Barone looked at his watch and shook his head. It was only five o'clock in the morning. They would have to wait another two hours before the Mass. From his place at the table he could see through the basement window that it was snowing in gusts outside. It wasn't going to be such a good day for a funeral.

"I knew I shouldn't have brought Michael," his sister said again.

Marie was pacing nervously just beyond the kitchen table, in the open area of the basement. A washing-machine and large sink occupied one corner. A coat rack and an old sofa the other. The cement floor was painted grey and dipped slightly into a covered drainage hole in front of the sink. The end of the linoleum marked the boundary of the kitchen. It was where their mother cooked all their meals. The more modern one upstairs was only used to entertain guests.

Joey sipped his coffee while observing his older sister. Earlier she had tried to get some sleep in her old room upstairs. But the noise of the crying had proved too bothersome, so she had decided to wait with him in the basement.

She was dressed very smartly in a black velour jacket and a brown tweed skirt. Her black hair came down in a coiled mass around her pinched face. Cleared of makeup, she had a strict aspect about her. He could remember her as a girl, slightly overweight, and rather aloof and distant, giving them the impression she was too good for the family. She had studied hard, gone to university and become so thin he hardly recognized her anymore.

He had put on his only dark suit, a knitted shirt without a tie, and slicked down his hair with water.

"He'll be all right," Joey said mechanically.

"There's no telling what sort of effect this will have on him. Even with the door closed he hasn't been able to sleep. He's a sensitive child."

"It won't be long now."

"I'll tell you, Joey, if I had known she was going to do this I'd never have brought him."

In the silence they could hear the sobs of grief issuing from their parents' bedroom on the first floor. Every so often the sobs gave way to moans, and then to deep-drawn wails that made him wince, as he did at the screeching of chalk. The crying had continued unabated all night.

Marie looked up at the ceiling, toward the bedroom. "Who are they anyway?" she said.

"Old friends of hers from the neighbourhood. The ones she still meets occasionally at church."

Marie shook her head and sighed. Upstairs, five black-draped old women along with his mother were seated around the bed and crying over the corpse of his father.

Marie had tried to prevent their mother from taking the body from the funeral home, but it was no use. Assunta wanted the body in the house the night before the funeral. She wouldn't listen to reason. There was no talking to her. Once the death had been pronounced after the long agony in the hospital, Assunta had taken over. In near hysterics she had immediately opened the windows of the hospital-room. It was to let his spirit out, she cried, as Joey was staring in awe at the wasted ravaged body of his father. Then, in her coarse black mourning clothes, she had directed operations. She told him whom to call, what clothes to wear and generally how to act. It wasn't by any means unusual, even though he was 28 and had been working at the plant for ten years. He was still unmarried and living with his parents. Whenever his father wasn't around he had been Assunta's mouthpiece with the English-speaking world.

The crying continued. Marie came back to the table to drink her coffee. She looked askance at him, rolling her eyes. He couldn't imagine what she was thinking except that she had probably come up from Toronto expecting a quiet funeral. She had never bargained for this. Neither had he for that matter. Their mother was old-country, but never to this extent. It was the first death in the family this side of the Atlantic. They hadn't even met their grandparents when they died. They were only kids. Assunta had received a letter and they hadn't seen her for a few days.

Joey couldn't say he knew Marie that well anymore. Since leaving for university she had rarely come back to visit. She had done well, except she hadn't gone far enough to become a professor, as he thought she would. Instead, she had married an English fellow who taught university, had Michael, and then became a math teacher. She had tried countless times to get him to visit Toronto, but the only time he went down was when she got married. He and Adamo went down without Assunta, who would have nothing to do with Marie's marriage away from the West End to some English stranger in a Protestant chapel. *Mi dispiace* he could remember Assunta saying on the phone, *ma non mi sento bene.* Whenever his mother didn't want to do anything she'd say it was because she didn't feel well. Marie must have known all along Assunta would never consent to such a long trip, even though it was for her wedding. Assunta had never gone beyond short Sunday car rides to the outskirts of the Sault. There had been ill-will between daughter and mother since Marie's high-school days. Joey didn't know who was more at fault, but Assunta's absence from the ceremony seemed to mean a serious breach. For the past year Marie had been separated from her husband Richard.

Sometime later the wailing stopped abruptly. Joey could smell smoke and the musty odour of old women. Then there was a high piercing shriek that reverberated throughout the house. Marie looked at him in alarm. They remained perfectly still. The shrieking sounded like nothing he had ever heard. It was something like an animal caught in a trap, knowing it was about to die. It went on and on, and he thought it would never end. He kept his eyes closed in pain.

When it stopped, Marie said casually, "That's certainly wakened Michael now."

Joey looked at her. There was a lump choking his throat. But he couldn't cry. He felt like reaching over the table and choking his sister until every tear in her body was squeezed out. They listened for the slightest noise.

"They've stopped," Marie said. "What time is it?"

It was close to six. The fridge suddenly sprang to life, startling both of them.

Presently they heard footsteps leaving the bedroom. The slow methodical shuffling was unmistakably his mother's. She paused at the head of the basement stairs, as if to collect herself. Then she called down to them.

"Jooo-eee...Maaa-reee-yiaaa...."

A strange look passed between him and his sister. It was as if they were kids again and Assunta was calling them to supper. Everything was fine. After eating maybe he'd go over to the school rink to play hockey. Marie would probably go over to Rita's as she always did when she was in grade eight. And Babbo was in the cantina working away at something or other at his workbench. The neighbourhood was alive with kids playing in the streets and he would never grow up if he could help it.

"Jooo-eee...Maaa-reee-yiaaa...*vieni vedere vostro Babbo.*"

But the voice didn't have the shrill assertive ring that used to carry through the neighbourhood. It was hoarse, and full of exhausted emotion.

"What's she saying?" Marie whispered to him.

But her eyes told him she already knew, that no matter how long she had been away she still understood enough Italian to know they were wanted to pay their last respects.

"Let's go," he said.

"I can't," Marie said, averting her face. "I went to the funeral home and I'll go to the church, but I won't be a party to this masquerade."

He was lost for words. In her fashionable jacket and tweed

skirt, thin to the point of being emaciated, she looked like someone from another world. Her wrists were like twigs that he could snap at will. Yet she had the power of language over him. He felt like a bumpkin in front of her when she was articulating those fancy phrases she had picked up in the big city.

"*...vostro Babbo,*" the hoarse voice repeated, this time in a painful gasp.

"Marie," he said, his voice close to breaking, "don't start anything now. She's your mother." He had wanted to say "he's your father." She looked at him for a minute, her eyes softening slightly as if pitying him.

"You've always done what they've wanted, haven't you?" she said.

"C'mon," he lowered his head. "Babbo's dead, Marie." He found it hard to breathe.

They went up the stairs together. Assunta stood at the top just under the light. He couldn't look up at her. The lump in his throat was so large he couldn't swallow.

When they reached the top no words were passed between them. He was afraid to make the slightest sound. His mother's look said it all. Her face, reddened and swollen with weeping, was a hideous mask. Her lips were bloodied and her hair dishevelled, as if she had been tearing at it. He couldn't look straight into her eyes. They had a crazed look about them that scared him. The past few months of his father's illness had affected her severely. She had become thinner than ever. It seemed her frame had slightly collapsed. She was hunched over. Her face had wrinkled badly. And there were permanent dark patches under her eyes that emphasized her martyred expression. She was undeniably an old woman now, he thought, as he towered above her. And the black dress, along with the heavy black stockings and the kerchief, seemed to suit her perfectly. When Marie had first seen her, the day after Babbo's death, she had asked him where Assunta could've gotten such an old dress.

"Probably from the old chest in the bedroom," he said.

"You mean the Hope Chest?" She sounded surprised.

"Where else could she have gotten it?"

It was Marie who actually came to call it the Hope Chest, he remembered. She meant the dowry and trousseau trunk their mother had brought over from the old country. Assunta called it a *bavulo* in dialect. According to her it contained her only possessions when she crossed the ocean. When he and Marie were kids Assunta used to tell them of the tradition in Novilara, her village home in Marche, of passing the *bavulo* from mother to daughter—when the daughter married or the mother died. It had gone through a couple of generations already, with the original brass handles and most of the original wood still intact. Marie used to think of it as her personal possession, even though it had always been kept locked in their mother's bedroom. Joey could remember Marie's determined efforts to find the key.

As kids they first had an inkling of how their parents came to be married through their quarrels. Some aspect would invariably come out in the heated exchanges. Later they were told the story by their father. Apparently Adamo had come to the new country from an Abruzzi village all alone before the war. He had heard of the job opportunities in Sault Ste. Marie from relatives of men who had already gone. To them the Sault, even though a small city in Northern Ontario, was *l'America*. If one were prepared to work one could obtain a house with running water—and maybe even a car. He had worked hard in the steel plant to become established, and then to buy a house. But he was getting on in years and anxious to start a family, so he had written to his parents after the war. Word had passed into a network of relatives. He had asked for someone who was not immature, and who would bear him good children. Somehow, through a mutual friend, Assunta had been included in the prospective list. She came from the adjacent province farther north. His parents would vouch for each selection with their lives. They had sent him a number of photographs, from which he selected three. He didn't know which one had consented until he saw her step off the train at the Sault Station.

Joey looked at his mother. It had been a long time since she had stepped off that train with her dowry trunk. And in all that time she had never ceased to puzzle him. He didn't know whether she had purposely refused to adapt to the new ways or if she was incapable of doing so. She was certainly stubborn. She had strange old-country customs that she insisted on maintaining even though they were primitive and embarrassing. Her drastic fluctuating moods were beyond him too. She was capable of laughing heartily one minute and lashing out in anger the next, as if she acted on pure impulse. He found it incredible that she still hadn't learned English. Thirty odd years here and all she had was the occasional word for telephone callers and tradesmen. Although she seemed to understand him and Marie well enough at times. It seemed she had gone from one Italian village in Marche to another one in Northern Ontario—the West End.

Joey couldn't say he had tried very hard in figuring her out, though. He only knew enough *dialetto* to get along with her on the most practical of levels. If anything more complicated had to be said he could only say it in English or stare at her in exasperation. Sometimes, if there was a difference of opinion he'd have to repeatedly shout the only phrases he knew. It was like stretching his meagre Italian vocabulary into all sorts of distortions. Usually the tone of voice or the facial expression had to suffice for his lack of words. He didn't have much faith in the words anyway. But if all else failed and his father wasn't there to help them, they simply couldn't communicate.

When they got to the front of the house, Marie started up the stairs instead of entering the bedroom.

"I want to check on Michael," she said. "I'll be down in a moment."

He gave her a sour look.

His mother had him by the arm. Either she needed his

support or she was afraid he'd leave also.

The old women were sitting around the bed, hunched over and staring at the floor. All he could hear was the wheezing sound of their heavy breathing. The scene had the air of something important having been settled. They were resting now after their ordeal, their faces withdrawn as their shoulders heaved with their laboured breathing. The two large candelabra placed at the head of the bed threw their shadows against the walls like hulks of stone. Other candles had been placed around the room as well. The place had an air of unreality.

Adamo was laid in his best dark suit and shoes in the middle of the bed, with rosary beads in his hands and flowers on either side of him. The clothes were too large for the body wasted by cancer. His face was powdered and made to look more like a street dandy than a factory worker. It seemed to have an expression of incredulity about it, as if he couldn't quite believe his working days were finally over. His hair was totally white now. He looked almost doll-like.

The sight made Joey wince. Somehow it wasn't right to remember his father in repose looking like some aged gigolo instead of the bricklayer he was.

The air was thick with the smell of wax and flowers. Joey could feel his heart pounding.

For a minute the black-draped figures sat still on either side of him. They had black shawls over their heads and looked grotesquely unnatural in the flickering light. Most were stout, with their thick legs splayed out. Two were lean and shrivelled, their small frames engulfed by their black clothes. They all displayed solemn trance-like expressions.

He could remember these Calabrese and Brutsese women when they'd come to visit his mother. They used to gaggle like geese long into the night, back in the old days when the neighbourhood was a going concern. All peasant women like his mother, they had brought their old-country existence with them to the West End. Now they had been dispersed by urban renewal, either following their families to whichever corner of the city they could find a new home or to one of the two old-age homes that had sprung up in the West End. Wherever they had ended up they still managed to get to Mount Carmel church in the mornings for their ritualistic Mass. Only the widow Angeline, who lived next door, had stuck it out on her own up to now. But she wasn't old-country enough to be with this group. Like a chorus of professional mourners, they could've stepped out of the middle ages. He remembered they mockingly used to call them Black Madonnas in the old days.

Without word they started to file out behind him. Someone put her hand on his shoulder. He flinched with revulsion.

"*Non perdere coraggio,* Joey," she said. "*Bisogna sempre sperare nell'aiuto del Signore.*"

Suddenly he was alone with the body. His mother had probably gone to prepare for Mass. He sat perfectly still. The walls flickered with light. His mother had put some of the candles on top of the dresser in front of the mirror. Above the bed hung the portrait of the Sacred Heart, its waxy surface glowing faintly in the light.

It was finally over, he thought. After all that suffering in the hospital, it was almost a relief to see his father in repose.

For a minute Joey looked closely at Adamo's face. It was still handsome in death, with the firm, clefted chin and the fine solid features. But he couldn't look for very long. The lump in his throat expanded painfully. He saw too much of himself in the dead body.

Too disturbed to look up again, he stared fixedly at the end of the bed, keeping his father's shoes in view. Somehow the way the toes were pointed outwards suddenly jarred his memory.

He saw Adamo running after him when he was a kid. He must have done something wrong, like playing hockey without permission. His father's belt was brandished as he waddled after him. "Run, run," he was saying. "If I ever catch you, *vigliacco. . . .*" Joey ran for his life out of the house and up the tracks where Adamo was no match for him. Then Adamo was walking toward the plant, his lunchpail in his hand, his head bowed. He walked like Charlie Chaplin. "You're not a kid anymore," he said, looking up at him. "You have to do something with your life. You can't play hockey all the time." Then he saw Adamo walk hesitantly toward their bench at the Memorial Gardens. His team had made the playoffs. The arena was packed with people. He turned his head away for the shame he felt. Adamo came up to him. His teammates looked away, embarrassed. "Joey," he said, putting his hand tentatively on his shoulder, "I'm sorry for hitting you." He looked around angrily to tell him to get lost. He had trespassed on his turf. But at that moment he saw that his father's eyes had moistened. His face expressed so much feeling that he was struck dumb.

Presently Marie came in and took one of the chairs vacated by the Black Madonnas. They sat in silence for a while. It was difficult to breathe in the room, even though the door had been left open. Joey was afraid to speak lest his voice break. He had fixed his eyes on his father's hands. They were gnarled and heavily callused. One finger had been squashed by a pile of bricks. Another had its nail split by a chisel. It didn't seem right for the rosary to be there. His father had very little use for religion. He railed against Father Sarlo constantly. Priests were parasites working off the labour of honest men. Church was for women. The only time you'd see him in a church was at Christmas, for the benefit of his family, and at his funeral, when he'd have no say in the matter.

"Mom's getting Michael ready," Marie finally spoke out. "I don't want him to see Babbo. Even Mom scares him."

She had only brought her son up once to see Adamo in the hospital. Their father was looking bad then. Michael had stood at the end of the bed looking shy and uncomfortable. Adamo had only smiled and said a few words. He didn't know his grandson well enough to be very affectionate.

"If you had brought him up more times..." Joey said.

"What?" she said, as if she hadn't heard him.

He didn't respond. She didn't belong in the room with him. It was he who had stayed. It was he who had visited the hospital. It was he who had lived in the house all these years while she was off getting educated, effacing all the marks of her Italian blood.

Marie said, "He doesn't look very much like Babbo, does he?"

He remained quiet, her self-assurance overpowering him. "The thing I remember most about him," she went on, as if Joey weren't there, "is the way we used to argue. I'd be washing the dishes and he'd still be at the dinner table and we'd talk about things I was learning in school. He'd get so flustered at times I thought he'd hit me. He picked up all these silly ideas at the plant and the Marconi Hall and I'd try to correct him and he'd say I only knew things from books. 'You're not a kid anymore,' he'd say. I don't think I've ever seen him reading anything, not even a newspaper. He never went past grade five and reading hurt his eyes, he said. And yet he took care of us the best he could, didn't he? I don't know, it was hard to know him. He was a secretive man in many ways. And so different from me. It's hard to believe he was my father."

"Babbo left me the house," Joey said, changing the topic abruptly and almost snapping at her.

She looked at him, surprised. "It's really Mom's," he added, "but Babbo told me to look after it. To only sell it to the city if I had to. Mom wouldn't know what to do."

They were talking in whispers, each staring at the body, only connected by the business of tying some loose ends. The city had wanted to expropriate their house for a while now. The old industrial neighbourhood had been chipped away piece by piece.

Marie seemed to accept the explanation. "What about Mom?" she said, her voice laden with meaning.

"I know," he said.

"What're you going to do?"

He couldn't get over the way she took things for granted so easily.

"I don't know," he shook his head.

"You've stayed long enough in the house, Joey," she said, her tone solicitous.

"I know."

"You've done all you could. You've got to think of yourself now."

He remained silent for a while, thinking of what she said. She was older by two years and had left home for all intents and purposes when she went to university ten years ago. For some reason he had stayed. Had not gone south to play Junior hockey. And then had not gone to university.

"Babbo said we should take care of her," he said, keeping his eyes on Adamo's hands, his voice so low he didn't think she had heard him.

Joey had thought he would wait until after the funeral to tell his sister, but this seemed as good a time as any. They weren't going to cry over the body like the old woman. They weren't going to pray either. And Marie seemed too uncomfortable with silence.

He recalled the time at the hospital. They were alone. Adamo had been told he didn't have much time left. His eyes were large with fear. "What about your Mamma, Joey?" he had said all of a sudden. "What's going to happen to her?" They had stared at each other for some time, the emotion flowing between them so painful that finally Joey had to avert his eyes.

Even when he had told Adamo about the letter from the Junior team down south, that they wanted him to try out, there had been very few words between them. Joey had been so joyous about it that he had automatically felt the whole world would be proud of him. It was an honour that up to that time few Sault boys had enjoyed. The scouts had seen him play and had confidentially told him there'd be no worry about making the team. And if he made the team, there'd be a good chance of playing professional hockey, which was his life-long dream. But his father had looked hurt beyond measure. His eyes downcast, his voice wavering, Adamo had said, "You want to leave home because of this?"

Turning to face his sister, he saw that her mouth was set in a thin line of annoyance.

"What do you mean, take care of her?" she said. Her voice was abrupt and hard.

"Take care of her, that's all," he said.

She looked back at him, her eyes dark and wary.

"What do you mean, 'we'?"

He turned away quickly, knowing what she meant. He was sorry he had mentioned it. It seemed blasphemous to go into such things with Adamo's body in front of them.

Staring at his father's hands, he tried to control himself. "She's your mother too," he said.

He could've sworn she gave a soft contemptuous laugh.

"Mother?" she said, as if it were a foreign word.

Joey sat glum and silent. In a few more minutes the hearse would arrive and they would put the decaying flesh of his father into a casket and bring it to the church and then to the cemetery and see it no more.

"Babbo," he said to himself, as if trying out the word for the first time. "What do we do if we can't pray or cry for you?"

"How can she be my mother if she's never had the slightest idea of who I was?" Marie was saying, mostly to herself, caught up in her own emotion. "We've never spoken the same language even. How can she be my mother? She's never had the least comprehension of what I was doing in school or what I wanted in life. All she did was cook and wash for me. And hit me a lot when I was a kid. There are no two people so different as we are. She's like a fossil. She's in the wrong time and the wrong country. So how can she be my mother? Tell me."

He saw that her lips were trembling. "Tell me, Joey," she went on, her voice breaking. "How can she be my mother?"

She was looking at Adamo and shaking her head. Soon her body started to quake and she was crying silently.

At that moment Joey sensed someone behind them. He turned slightly in his chair and saw his mother standing in the doorway and regarding them. There was a resigned, aggrieved expression on her face. Immediately he wondered how much she had overheard—and if she had overheard how much she had understood. Although she didn't speak English she did know enough words from the context to get the general drift at times.

But she didn't say a word. Marie noticed her and gave a little start. The three of them remained still. It was like a tableau in which each was trying to see what the other would do. Joey noticed how grief had fixed lines in her face. For some reason she had taken off her dentures and her collapsed mouth gave her an even more piteous and agonized look. For a second he thought she was deeply wounded. But looking more closely he saw it was fear. It was the same look his father had given him in the hospital.

"Mamma?" he said, frightened for her.

But she didn't respond. He felt his eyes getting moist as he held her gaze. In spite of the fact that all Marie had said about her was true, he felt something deeper and more important inside him know that this was irrelevant. That this frail woman was closer to him than any other human being. He had to avert his eyes. He was crying for the first time.

From this angle he noticed that the Hope Chest just behind the door had recently been opened. The stacks of *Grand Hotel* that had always rested on top had been removed and the coverlet had been pushed aside. A piece of cloth was sticking out from the side.

Joey looked at Marie, but she didn't seem to have noticed it. Her face was fighting back the tears as she regarded the small figure in the doorway. There was an open imploring aspect about the stare, as if she were waiting for some sort of sign. But Assunta made no move toward them.

When they heard the hearse stop in front of the house, she slipped away.

After the Mass it was the custom in the West End for the funeral cortège to take the deceased around the neighbourhood for the last time.

Joey drove the limousine behind the hearse. Michael was in front with him, while Marie and his mother were in the back. Except for some sniffling, Assunta had been quiet in the church. Her face was completely obscured by a veil. Marie was looking sullenly out of the window. Michael had his winter parka on and sat extremely still. It was apparent he had been deeply affected by the past few days. Joey knew him as a quiet boy, with sandy hair and Marie's dark, brooding eyes.

It was a cold windy day. Snow was still falling in gusts, which swept across the newly ploughed streets leaving small dunes in front of the snowbanks. The exhaust from the hearse jumped out quickly into the cold northern air. They could expect below-zero temperatures for the rest of January. Joey could recall long winters in the Sault when 30 below was not unusual. When he used to play on the outdoor rink at McFadden school his nose would often get so white that he'd be afraid to touch it lest it fall off.

As they started off Michael looked up at Joey, his eyes large and playful.

"I know where *nonno* is," he said.

"Be quiet, Mikey," Marie quickly said.

Joey saw the boy's face crumple. He looked straight ahead.

From Our Lady of Mount Carmel they went down Cathcart toward the steel plant. A few houses still stood in this part of the neighbourhood. They had been neglected so long, however, that they were in various states of disrepair. Built close together at the sidewalk, they had enclosed verandahs and fenced-in backyards with rickety sheds or garages. The Italian ones were easily distinguishable in the summer by their vegetable gardens, while the others had overgrown grass. They all had that imitation brick siding that had long been faded by its exposure to the steel-plant air. Joey knew it was only a matter of time before these too were torn down.

The diamond where he used to play baseball every Sunday after Mass was no more than a deserted field with waist-high grass. In the heyday of the neighbourhood it was the location of the High-Line bridge that crossed the width of the plant and connected the West End to the other industrial area of the city—Bayview. Most of the old-timers used to tell him it was the destruction of the High-Line and the erection of the International bridge joining the United States to Canada that had spelled the end of the neighbourhood. Both the Canadian and the American cities had the same name and were known for their Seaway canals that made Lake Superior accessible to the rest of the world. The International bridge came over both Sault canals from the south and cut a big chunk out of the heart of the Italian neighbourhood. Once city planners saw what the American tourists were seeing as they came over the bridge, urbal renewal came in and levelled the eyesores to make room for apartment buildings and old-age homes.

The cortège turned down West Street toward No. 2 Gate. They were moving very slowly. Joey kept his eye on the hearse while looking out at the familiar surroundings. As they neared the gate the large flaming A logo of the plant came into view. His eye was taken by the way it dominated the skyline. In bright red, with white flames passing through its centre, it was tilted slightly on its supports and rose like a huge neon sign above the two brick entrances.

He wondered how many times his father had walked underneath that tilted A to get to the masonry change-rooms. And back to punch out. The countless shifts that comprised half of his waking life. With his black lunchpail and his peaked cap, and his head slightly bowed to hide the dispirited look on his face.

"It's all so changed," Marie abruptly spoke up. "I used to hate it so much. Now I just feel sad about it. Babbo should've moved out a long time ago."

Her words grated on his ears. All words would be useless now, he felt. They would draw attention to themselves and away from what they should have been feeling down in the pit of themselves where no words lay.

"Do you remember, Joey, the time the Queen passed by here?" Marie went on, merely using his name out of expediency. "When they built the Gate and the sign? In that open carriage of hers? Everyone was lined up on Queen Street and they had to hide the eyesores, especially the old junkyard. The streets were decked in streamers. Even commemorative coins were made. The Queen was to see the Sault's most prestigious institution—the steel plant. But she had to pass through a settlement of semi-subdued Italians outside to get to the fort inside. I stood over there against the fence of that garden watching—and thinking we were living in quite a place to have the Queen of the World visit us. But she was so small, I remember...small and wax-like as she waved, bringing tradition to a small back-garden neighbourhood in a backwoods province of an inconsequential country. How could the southern Italians ever have come to Northern Ontario? It's beyond me."

Slowly the cortège turned down Queen and away from the plant gate. Joey caught the flaming A in the rearview mirror.

It was his father's last exit, he thought. And his father had often talked of a pension. Now it seemed he had finally got it. Quite a pension at that, too. You were put in a box with a memento of your services and laid into the earth to retire forever. You would lie there soaking in the dark, and your flesh would tan to the colour of your bones, and then the box would rot and you'd be the pieces of stone that held up the earth for others to walk on. You start as a working man and you are forever a working man.

Babbo would never complain, though, Joey thought. It was his job. Everyone had a job to do, he used to say. You're not a kid anymore. You can't play hockey all your life.

No, it wasn't the Queen of England parading down the Sault's main street. It was a simple working man, as Adamo used to call himself. And there was no-one on the street to wave goodbye. No fellow workers. No company men. They were all in the fort carrying on business as usual.

As they turned up James Street Marie spoke up again.

"Fitting, isn't it? The confectionery store still there. The senior citizens' home right where the old pool-hall used to be. The West End was always for kids and old people anyway."

James Street...where he used to stand on the corner with his buddies eating bag after bag of sunflower seeds and chucking the shells onto the sidewalk. Horsing around. Talking about nothing in particular. Just good to be out, acting as if you owned the street. Then going to Tony's and shooting a few. Or to the pinball game at Joe's. There was always some form of game to occupy their time. As kids, if it wasn't marbles or tossing baseball cards against the wall or kick the can, it was going to the ball park at the head of the street or the hockey rink at McFadden. James Street was their headquarters, though. It was the two confectionery stores—Pat's and Joe's—where they bought comics and liquorice and pack after pack of bubble-gum cards. It was Pee-Pee's where they always went to get secondhand skates or running-shoes. And the grocery stores—Ciotti's and Scarfone's—where they could swipe fruit from the sidewalk stalls. And Jerry's Diner where the guys met over cokes to talk about the latest sports "pheenom" or brought their first dates for an ice cream cone and thus claimed them for life. And the other places—the clothing stores and barber shops, the two hardware stores where they could get mitts and balls, the taxi-stand with the tarty dispatch woman, and the two taverns with that awful smell coming out of the air vents.

It was only two blocks long, but somehow it had been their

whole world.

Now there were only a few parking-lots and highrise apartments. No more kids on the street. No more ball park and school rink. There were only remnants left—remnants of the decayed body that had tanned to its bones.

The cortège turned right on Albert, where it cut James in half, and proceeded eastward to pass their house for the last time. The old McFadden public school was on their right, now only used for administrative offices. Then the smaller of the two senior citizens' homes. A simple brick building. Then the widow Angeline's house. And their own house.

Joey looked at it sadly. His father had worked on it off and on almost all his life. It appeared very vulnerable now that Adamo was gone. With its imitation grey siding and the awning over the front door and the cement steps with the black ornamental iron railing. Joey had lived there all his life. As a kid he used to think it was the best location in the West End. Right beside the tracks that cut through the middle of the neighbourhood and crossed the canal to the Michigan side. It was close to everything. The outdoor rink at McFadden. The ball park. James Street. The Catholic elementary school he attended just down from the tracks. And the tracks themselves that brought him to the river and canal in no time.

But later in life he had found it was close to the steel plant as well.

As they were passing the house Assunta suddenly gave out a series of shrill wails that made him jump in his seat. He looked around and the car lurched to a stop right in the middle of the tracks. She seemed hysterical. Marie immediately reached over to comfort her, but she cringed and nestled back into the corner. Michael started crying in fear.

"Keep driving!" Marie shouted at him in alarm.

He tried to breathe evenly. Slowly he got the car going again. They went over the tracks and the cortège resumed its course. Marie reached over the front seat and comforted her son. “It’s all right, Michael. It was only your grandmother. It’ll all be over soon.”

In the rearview mirror he saw the crumpled form of his mother. She was crying softly into her hands. She had scared the wits out of him. There was no telling what she would do. Clearly Adamo’s death meant something to her that they had no way of knowing.

Just then Marie’s face loomed over him in the mirror. Their eyes met for a moment. There was a strange look in hers. He couldn’t tell whether she was pitying him or asking for his forgiveness.

Whatever it was, though, he knew it would be him alone who would look after the old woman in the back seat.

z

Standing with her mother on the front steps of the house, Marie watched the Festa procession come up Albert over the tracks. It was heading for James Street and then back to the church. Parishioners were lined up on both sides of the street. It was a bright Saturday in May, with a light breeze ruffling the banners of the parish.

After the banners came the Knights of Columbus in their tails and sashes, with their scabbards sticking out the back. She recognized them as leading men of the parish, proud and dignified in their bearing. Then came a whole stream of school kids in white shirts and blouses chanting the rosary with military precision. Some faces were set in piety while others were clearly embarrassed. These were followed by the altar boys. The younger ones carrying candles and the older ones swinging censers that filled the air with a sweet aroma. Father Sarlo was behind in his finest array—brocaded white cape and matching biretta—walking imperiously and sprinkling people with holy water. His face pious and lordly, his head bowing with the movements of the sprinkler as if acknowledging everyone in turn. Then the centre of the procession itself. The bier holding the large statue of Our Lady of Mount Carmel which took four men to carry. Our Lady in powder-blue and white holding a scapular medal in her outstretched hand, and dollar bills pasted like wreaths around her neck. People every so often going up to the bier to deposit their offerings. And at the end of the line the black-draped old women of the parish with rosaries dangling from their hands, following the chants of Hail Marys and Glory Bes of the school kids in their particular fashion. Their lips moving in prayer, but the sound scarcely audible. Their eyes vacuous and long-suffering. Her mother beside her reciting the Hail Marys one after the other, her face dark and fervent.

"Santa Marie, madre di Dio, prega per noi peccatori..."

Then stepping onto the sidewalk as the bier was passing.

"Marietta, go in the house," she said in Italian. "Hurry, get my purse."

Always being treated like a kid. Close to sixteen and almost a senior at Collegiate, but treated like a kid, pure and simple, who existed merely to do the housework and learn all the female chores. As if she were being groomed to be another devoted Italian wife.

This is how you knead the dough, Marietta. And keep it going so that it'll come out strong and even.

You have to take care of the garden like a baby, changing its diapers, feeding it, having it close to your heart all the time so that it'll hear your heartbeat.

All this mortar from your father's work clothes has to be scraped off by hand first. Then two washings so that they're clean as new.

When she came back with the purse Assunta took out a $5 bill. Her mother had put on a new print dress that morning. It was light blue, with white flowers. When she bent over you could see the garters just below her knees. Her greying straggly hair was tied back in a bun. And she had put just a touch of lipstick on. For some reason she became very excited over parish or neighbourhood acivities like Festa Day.

"Go and give it to Our Lady," Assunta handed her the bill. "Go on."

Marie looked at the money and then at her mother, as if she hadn't heard.

"Hurry, Maria. They're moving past."

She was wearing an old sweatshirt and house slippers. Her hair, which had been bobbed recently in the latest style, was in a mess. She searched in her quickly dwindling Italian vocabulary for some phrase that would convey her wishes with a measure of dignity. But all she could find were the pat phrases of her childhood.

"No, Ma, I can't. I don't want to. People, they see me."

"Yes, *stupida,* they're supposed to. Hurry, you're losing your chance."

"You go." She stuck the money out defiantly.

"*Ma, che cosa?*" her mother made a gesture of incomprehension. Her mouth hung slack and slightly open. Her eyebrows arched up into neat little furrows.

Marie turned her face away in annoyance. Unexpectedly, she was pushed into the street. It felt as if she had been struck across the mouth. Completely disarmed, she looked around her as if lost. Her face had flushed a deep crimson.

"Go, hurry, Marietta," her mother said playfully. "Put it in the donation basket, hurry."

She had to run forward to catch up to the bier. All she was trying to make out were the donation baskets along the sides. The old women kept their eyes downcast. Her slippers felt like huge wooden clogs. As soon as she got within range she dropped the bill over the basket. Somehow it missed and fell to the street. The wind started to blow it away.

One of the men carrying the bier, the lanky shoe salesman from Pee-Pee's who had an idiotic face, snorted with laughter.

She felt the eyes of the entire West End on her, just waiting to see her humiliate herself further. For a second, pride prevented her from going after the money. But it was too much to let go. Awkwardly she ran after it. Someone in the crowd suddenly stepped out and stomped on it in an exaggerated show of bravado. A few people clapped and cheered. Even Father Sarlo seemed amused. She made a feeble attempt to smile, grabbed the money, and walked back to the bier.

Looking up at the statue, Marie saw the aloof expression on the Blessed Virgin's face, serene and indifferent to the humiliations of ordinary mortals. It seemed the perfect pose to thumb at the West End. But she knew she'd have to leave in order to learn it.

Stung to the point of tears, she set her face and walked resolutely toward the house. But before she could get safely in to hide herself Assunta yelled out to her. It was too loud to be ignored.

"*Maaa-reee-yia, vieni qui!*"

It was just like the times Assunta called her to dinner from the doorstep, screaming out her name at the top of her lungs like a vulgar washerwoman. Sometimes she felt there was no end to the indignities she had to suffer being the daughter of Italian parents.

"Come to the Mass with me. Come, Marietta."

People were joining the end of the Festa procession to attend the Mass. The Black Madonnas were being engulfed by the younger, more colourfully dressed women. Some had even managed to coax their men to come along with them, dragging them by the arm or scolding them unabashedly on the street.

Marie stepped up to Assunta. She was furious. It wasn't enough that she had been pushed. Now this. To be treated so thoughtlessly. She had only come out to see if the procession had changed since she had participated in it during grade school. Her mother had come up to her while she was sunning herself in the back. She had been trying to burn her skin enough to hide some of the red blotches that had broken over her face. Now it felt as if her mother had scratched them raw.

She knew it was no use saying anything. The words would only start deep down in her stomach as convincing English and plop out of her mouth like marbles in childish Italian.

But the expression on her face had no effect on her mother whatsoever. Her mother asked her again to come to the Mass.

"Go yourself, Ma," Marie was forced to speak.

"What's the matter with you, uh? You don't believe in God anymore? You sin too much? It's Festa. Everybody be there."

"I don't want to go. You go."

"My daughter, she's too good to go to church now? Is that it? You learn that in your books? They teach you not to go to church? Have you no shame?"

"Ma, I don't want to argue. Just go and leave me alone."

"Please, Marietta. We just walk with these people. Rita, she still go to church. Everybody go. You can't stop going to church. What's going to happen to you?"

Assunta grabbed her by the arm, trying to draw her into the line heading for the church. Violently she pulled her arm free.

"No, I said!"

Her mother's face twisted in pain, as if she had been struck across the face. She looked about to cry, her face totally incredulous, her eyes moistening. But in a moment she had stiffened again, her face assuming its usual martyred expression.

"You're such a weight on me, Marietta. I don't know what to do with you. You're such a shame and a disgrace...."

And on she went. *Vergogna* this and *disgrazia* that. She couldn't believe a daughter of hers would ever stop going to church. It was an unpardonable sin. What were they teaching her at that public school? She'd have to speak to Adamo to send her to the girls' Catholic school. *Mannaggia America* to have produced a daughter like her.

But the procession was fast receding around James Street

and she had to leave. Shaking her head in disbelief, she hurried off with a final look of wearied disapproval. They'd have to talk later.

In the afternoon Marie headed for James Street herself. Rita had called, asking her to come straight over to Guzzo's Dry Goods. There was something she had to tell her.

Marie wouldn't have dreamed of going to James Street on Festa Day otherwise. There was a sidewalk sale going on. It was all part of the day-long festivities that would culminate in the carnival games and fireworks display behind the Marconi Hall later that night.

Ever since going to high school, the West End was becoming more and more intolerable to her. For some reason she found almost everything about it either obnoxious or trite. The Italian women shopping at the grocery stores, feeling or smelling every little piece of food. The stupidity and boorishness of the street kids, who made loud vulgar remarks at her. The old dingy houses reeking of pasta sauce and threadbare linoleum. The stinking fumes coming from the steel plant and the Abitibi Pulp and Paper Mill.

Not to mention the behavior of her mother.

James Street was a buzz of activity. Traffic had been closed off at either end. Masses of people were strolling about, either checking the merchandise on the sidewalks or going up and down the street. Large Italian women with their dime-store dresses and huge shopping-bags patrolled the wares. Most of the men had their ill-fitting Sunday suits on and were talking in little rings in the middle of the street. Salesmen were shouting. The women were haggling over prices. Young kids were causing mischief on their bikes and getting cursed at. The older ones were in groups walking up and down like the true owners of the street. Marie could hear Italian music coming from a scratchy phonograph record.

She made a dash for Guzzo's just up the street.

Miss Guzzo was tending to her merchandise on the sidewalk. She was a stout middle-aged spinster with a few moles on her cheeks who played the organ at Mount Carmel. She gave Marie a dirty look as she stepped inside the store, knowing full well she wasn't there to shop. Miss Guzzo was probably the best dressed woman in the neighbourhood. She had overly fastidious mannerisms and a certain amount of hauteur, all of which tended to clash with her unattractive body.

Guzzo's was a very small shop and always smelled of the bolts of cloth that protruded from shelves all along one wall. There were a few dresses and blouses on hangers in the middle. And along the far wall were all sorts of religious statues, rosaries, missals, and pictures. When Marie made her first communion her mother had brought her to Guzzo's to buy a small white prayer book. When she passed grade seven she got a large St. Joseph Daily Missal.

After finishing with a customer Rita came over and looked out the window.

Rita Giunti was her last remaining friend in the neighbourhood. She was dark complexioned, with small features and curly brown hair. She had a sort of cherubic prettiness. Since getting her job at Guzzo's she had taken to wearing pleated navy skirts, with white blouses and saddle shoes. She had also assumed an air of self-importance that somehow didn't suit her.

They had both gone to Collegiate instead of the girls' Catholic high school. Rita was actually too Italian, though. Marie would've discarded her long before, except that she was finding it hard to make friends with the more popular girls at Collegiate. With their unquestioning sense of themselves and their cliquishness they made a formidable group. And she was too proud to fall into line by playing up to them. It meant joining the same clubs at school and gushing over the same boys. Or doing the fashionable thing, which she actually didn't mind doing, except she'd die if they ever snubbed her. They all read *Seventeen* and *Miss Teen* and were so excited about becoming a woman. Rita, even with her newly acquired airs, was down to earth, dependable—and definitely not as popular as the others.

What had perhaps stung the most, though, was that at the few school dances they had attended Rita had been asked to dance at least four times. While she had been entirely ignored. It was positively humiliating. What could they see in Rita they didn't see in her? Rita told her she was too stand-offish. But she just couldn't smile idiotically and go gaga whenever a boy came within range. Once Rita had even made an offhand remark about her weight.

"The waist is very important," she had said. "If you have no waist, you have nothing else. That's what Miss Guzzo says."

From the same Miss Guzzo who was all waist herself. She could stick whatever Miss Guzzo told her.

But when Marie had exposed her waist to the mirror that same night she noticed that it did indeed hide everything else in a sort of lumpy mass. Her weight had always been a problem. Yet she had only tried to do something about it after starting her periods. Menstruation had made her feel unclean inside. Somehow it compelled her to improve her outward appearance. It was as if she had to hide her uncleanliness in a bright shiny vessel. There had been some improvements since then, but not nearly enough to satisfy Miss Guzzo's standards.

And if that wasn't enough, her complexion had started to break out in the past year.

She had cried bitterly that night in front of the mirror and determined to diet herself into a figure that would satisfy anyone's standards. She had the hips and the bust. All she had to do was get rid of the part in between.

But she had again underestimated the obstacle of her mother.

Assunta Barone was an absolute tyrant at the dinner table. Marie didn't know how she came to be that way or why, but it had been the case ever since she could remember. The table was like her theatre of operations and her rules were unquestioned. Whatever was put on the table had to be eaten. Ordinarily this wouldn't have been a problem except Assunta always managed to cook more than was needed. If dinner was for four she cooked for six. If for six, there was food enough for eight. And woe to the person who didn't eat his full portions. She badgered all during the meal—and even went so far as to put the food up to their mouths. Nothing escaped her eye. She sat imperiously, often neglecting her own food, and anticipated their every move. She directed operations as if managing a war game.

Mangia this and that, she'd say. *Non è bastanza.* Nothing was ever enough. Marie, you haven't eaten enough. How can you have eaten enough? Here, have some more. If you don't eat you'll get sick. You don't know the blessings you have. Only sparrows eat like that. And on and on.

And when Marie started her diet, refusing to let her mother ladle the pasta onto her plate, and taking small portions of everything, she was immediately accused of being *pazza,* crazy. Assunta looked stunned for a moment, then hurt—as if some private had rebuked her. If she wasn't crazy she must be ill then. Assunta came around the table to feel her forehead. That had to be it. Or she had been influenced by the English and their stupid eating habits. Or she was doing it merely out of spite to hurt her mother. Yes, that had to be it, she went on in dialect. Her poor mother didn't slave away in the kitchen to be treated so shabbily. Her own daughter, an *ingrata*—ungrateful for all they had done for her. Adamo didn't go to work to put food on the table so that it would be left uneaten.

As it was, Marie could only stick it out for five more days. It was just too difficult. Assunta badgered her not only during meals, but every minute of the day. She kept warning how she'd fall down from weakness. Or not have enough strength to do her homework. Or that she always looked sickly and pale. To the point where she was shorn of her defences. If she didn't have a nervous breakdown from not eating, Marie concluded, she'd certainly have one from her mother's constant harassment.

And so she had resumed her regular eating habits. She was never particularly athletic. Her lumpy waist continued to be a source of embarrassment.

All through grade nine she hadn't showered after gym class. She positively loathed those girls who would flauntingly walk to the shower cubicles in the nude. In the past year she took to draping a towel around her and only discarding it in the cubicle.

As Rita leaned closer to her she was inundated with perfume. "It's called *French Mist,*" Rita had confided to her a couple of weeks ago. "I bought it at Woolworth's. Miss Guzzo says a lady should always smell ladylike."

"Guess what?" she now said gleefully.

"You've been voted Festa Queen," Marie said with a straight face.

"Smarty-pants. Anne's giving a party tonight at her place."

Anne Vernelli, a friend from grade school, was third-generation Italian. Her parents allowed her to give parties—with boys and all.

"So?"

"So, she says. As if her appointment book was completely filled. Hardy-harr-harr."

Rita made a face that said she was doing the greatest favour in the world for somebody who was too dumb to appreciate it.

"So," Rita said, speaking with childish glee, "she came in here earlier and invited me to come."

Marie didn't betray any emotion. "So, what else is new?"

"You're invited too, silly."

The lack of interest made Rita even more determined to excite her. Out of the corner of her eye she kept a lookout for Miss Guzzo.

"Even Renzo is going to be there," Rita said, her eyebrows arching slightly.

Marie kept her nose up. "My interest in Renzo Lepera can be summed up in one word—nil."

Rita smiled at her. "C'mon, Marie, he's not so bad. He's changed quite a bit, I hear."

Ever since grade school she was supposed to be after Renzo. It seemed to have been decided by circumstances and availability rather than preference. Renzo, immature and pudgy, had been an absolute zero. She could only remember being with him twice. Once when she had found herself on a swing beside him at the park. Another time at a matinee at the Princess Theatre. She and Rita and a few of the other girls had found themselves surrounded by some of the boys. Renzo had somehow ended up sitting beside her. She had almost died. The Princess was notorious for Saturday matinee necking sessions. Renzo had mumbled a hello and what a good movie it was. She had made some inarticulate sound. Some of the others were giggling behind her. She had spent the whole double feature stiff in expectation. But Renzo was as shy as she was. He had been content simply to press his shoulder against hers and leave it at that.

From these two meetings her name was linked in every sort of amorous intrigue with the yo-yo of the class. She was greatly relieved when they went to separate high schools. Renzo went to the boys' college on the hill. Surprisingly, she had heard a few good things about him since then. He had taken up gymnastics and blossomed. She was curious to see how much he had changed. It must've been over two years since she had seen him last.

Marie put as much disdain as she could into her voice.

"That was all grade school stuff anyway. I can't imagine how you can still be interested in that sort of thing."

Rita smiled. "Yeah, but the boys have grown up since then. And I haven't seen very many boys beating at your door. You really should do something about your skin, Marie. Miss Guzzo says..."

"Oh, stop it! Always Miss Guzzo this and Miss Guzzo that.

Are you her protégé or something? Look at her out there. She's an old maid."

Rita was pouting. "At least I got a job," she said, turning her face away. "I just tried to do you a favour. Anne hadn't even thought of asking you, if you want to know the truth. I asked her if you could come with me." She shrugged. "I'm going anyway—if you want to or not."

Marie decided to ask her father about the party after dinner as she was doing the dishes. Assunta and Joey were upstairs watching TV. Since getting their first set four years ago it seemed to be on continuously from noon to midnight. Assunta claimed it soothed her, although she scarcely understood what was being said. All Joey seemed to do these days was watch TV and play sports. He was growing fast and was already as tall as Adamo. His light hair had darkened and become curlier. His face was sinking into the hard lines and clefts of his father.

Assunta had been quiet during dinner, but Marie hadn't failed to notice the sidelong glances she had given Adamo.

"How was work today, Babbo?" she said, her back to him.

He sat at the table with his coffee and wine bottle, quiet and pensive as usual after his shift. She had seen him laying bricks for the house chatting away to Joey like crazy. His hands moving quickly. Chopping the bricks in half with quick deft movements. Trowelling the mortar. His eyes deadly serious, yet the rest of his face happy as he worked on the house. When he had nothing to do, however, he tended to be taciturn and morose. He was animated enough when friends came over to visit and he had a chance to speak Italian. His English was slow and halting. They'd get into the occasional heated exchange over politics and ideas. But he was usually reserved with her, saving his more personal feelings for Joey.

"Oh, not bad," he said.

Marie tried to get him to talk about his work. He only mentioned having to line the inside of a furnace. As soon as she brought up the party there was a strained pause in the conversation.

"It's like a reunion, Babbo. I just found out about it today from Rita. Can I go?"

Instead of answering quickly he cleared his throat, the usual mannerism when he was uncomfortable.

"Your mother told me about this morning," he said, his tone reproving.

"That was nothing, Babbo. It's not even Sunday." She kept washing the dishes, knowing the inevitable was coming.

"Your mother, she told me you stopped going to church on Sundays too. Is that right?"

Quickly she snapped, "You don't go, Babbo."

"That's not important."

"It is too!"

"Maria, watch your mouth!"

She turned to face him, but he kept his eyes on the coffee mug. She knew it was easier for them to talk when they weren't looking at each other.

She went back to the dishes. "I try to go as much as I can. Sometimes I don't wake up in time, that's all."

"But you don't want to wake up sometimes too, uh? I hear your mother yelling at you on Sundays. This is important to her, Maria. You can't stop going to church. You're not a kid anymore."

"Oh, Babbo...."

She had to promise him she'd make a better effort in the future before he'd agree to the party. But she had to get Assunta's permission too. And when she went upstairs to sit on the sofa chair opposite her mother, Assunta wouldn't even look at her. They were watching re-runs of an old situation-comedy. Every so often Assunta would ask Joey about the particulars of the plot and he would snap out his responses impatiently.

"Why don't you learn English, Ma," Joey said, irritated by the constant interruptions.

"*Per amor di Dio,* Joey, *abbi pazienza.*"

"Oh, c'mon," he scoffed, refusing to speak Italian.

After allowing a little time for Assunta to cool down, Marie patiently went over the conversation with Adamo. Her mother kept her eyes firmly on the set.

"Ma, can I go?" she pleaded in Italian. "Please."

Joey lost his patience again. "How can I listen with all this racket going on?"

"Oh, shut up," she snapped at him.

"Shut up yourself."

"Take a long walk on a short pier, will you."

"Take one yourself."

"Ma...."

Assunta looked at her angrily. "When you go to the church, then you can go to the party."

"Oh, Ma, you don't understand."

As she was trying to explain Joey turned the volume up to make his point. Marie had to practically shout above the din. This party was important to her, she said. Was she asking too much to just enjoy herself for once? Joey could do whatever he wanted, but she was still being treated like a child. Couldn't she at least see she had grown up. Did she have to stand naked in front of her to make her see? If she couldn't go, she'd starve herself to death. Then she'd show her. Her mother would be sorry then.

To all of which Assunta turned a deaf ear.

Finally Joey exploded in a temper tantrum and there was bedlam.

Marie ran out of the room. Instinctively she turned into her parents' bedroom at the bottom of the stairs, closed the door, and threw herself on the bed where she sobbed her heart out. It was just too unfair. Her mother was an illiterate peasant. And even worse—a mail-order bride. Ordered and bought like a piece of furniture. She couldn't understand a thing. She probably milked cows all her life. How could fate have been so cruel? That she had to be the offspring of such a contemptible woman. And had to suffer through more agonizing years of living under the same roof with her. It was so unfair.

Presently she got up and surveyed the room.

"I hate you," she said out loud.

There was no answer. In a blind fury she began to search for the key to the Hope Chest. First the bottom drawers of her mother's dresser. Going through each item to make sure it wasn't lodged in the folds. Then the top drawer with its hoardings of trinkets and old jewellery. And the good jewellery box in front of the mirror. All the overcoat pockets in the detached wooden wardrobe. As well as every other possible hiding place. In the same order and with the same thoroughness as the countless other times. It was now a blind habit more than anything else.

At the beginning it must have been pure curiosity to see the contents of the dowry chest. Put there undoubtedly by the story her mother had told her on the few occasions when she was communicative. How her own mother had given the chest to her before she left her village. That it wasn't to be opened till she was actually married in the new country. How she had travelled by train across Italy to Naples, and then boarded a boat and landed in Halifax—journeying all the while with the key safely hanging from her neckchain beside *Gesù Cristo*. How that fact more than any other had sustained her throughout that harrowing journey. All those different people. The outside world so wonderful and at the same time so scary because she had never been very far outside her village before that. And she wouldn't soon go so far again. How she had kept thinking of opening the wooden box and discovering all the treasures her mother had promised her. Treasures with which she could start a new life and raise a family. Treasures that would make her future husband value her above anyone else in the world.

Marie used to picture a trunk full of Spanish coins and jewellery, enough to buy a king's ransom.

At first she had wanted to find out what her mother was worth. Somehow that had passed into a curiosity over her own worth. It intrigued her that a woman could be equated with the contents of a trunk.

Later it was the pure obstinacy to outwit her mother. Assunta had found such a good hiding place for the key that she was at her wits' end. At times Marie even tried to catch Assunta adding to the Hope Chest when she made a seemingly unwarranted purchase. But all she ever saw changing were the stacks of *Grand Hotel* and the new coverlets adorning the outside.

In the past few years, however, the curiosity and the obstinacy had been greatly diluted by what she had come to realize about her mother. The revelation that she was a mail-order bride was the first blow. If anything could cast doubt on her value it was certainly that. Then gradually being ashamed of Assunta's failure to adapt to the new country. Not picking up the language. Remaining so blatantly old-country with her vulgar ways. Like still keeping a chamber pot under her bed at night. Or yelling at the top of her voice when she was angry. Or chattering like a magpie when her friends came to visit.

As the value of her mother decreased in her eyes so did the value of the Hope Chest.

Marie knew only the barest details of Assunta's life in the old country. She hadn't even been able to find the village in Marche on the map. Assunta's sister Pia, who had a daughter called Marisa, lived on a farm just below the village. Assunta had Adamo write a letter every two months to Pia. It was always addressed *Novilara, Provincia di Pesaro, Marche.* When Assunta received her letter from Pia it would be an occasion of great joy, which she would never share with anyone. She'd always read the letters alone and they'd never be seen again.

Finally giving up the search, Marie went upstairs to prepare for the party. She'd sneak out of the house and take the consequences later. She didn't know why she wasted so much time on such childish behavior. She and her mother were as different as night and day.

Looking at herself in the mirror, she felt a pang of injustice once again. Her complexion was getting worse with each passing day. Even the cosmetics she had learned about from reading magazines seemed ineffective. How could it be possible, she asked herself, that ugly blotches should suddenly materialize and disfigure the only part of her that she had in any way been proud of? She had watched the coming of the catastrophe with a sinking heart. And there was no-one to help her—or even to talk to her. At times in the past year she had lain in bed waiting for sleep with tears silently running down her cheeks, feeling entirely helpless against the trap of circumstances.

Other girls had told her about how their mothers spoke to them like friends or big sisters, taking such things entirely for granted. It seemed too hard to believe. Marie recalled how she had been so unprepared for her first period. She had heard some vague things from her friends, but when the first full one came upon her she was disgusted with herself and cried alone in the bathroom the whole afternoon of the school day. She had to ask her grade-school teacher what to do. Miss Patterson had given her a long lecture about the reproductive system, sanitary pads, and love. Marie could have kissed her hand in gratitude.

Later in the evening Marie managed to sneak out of the house unnoticed. But the party was a fiasco. Renzo didn't even remember her name. He was sitting alone when she and Rita approached him. As soon as she saw him she was amazed by the way he had changed. In two short years he had been transformed into a tall, hard-muscled young man whose body seemed to glow with vitality. His face was very handsome and he appeared more friendly than she had ever known him. Her only thought was how gorgeous he had become—while she had only changed for the worse.

Boldly Rita went up to him as he got up.

"Renzo Lepera," she said in mock recognition.
"Rita Giunti," his face lit up.
"You used to call me Moonface, remember?"
He laughed. "Yeah, but you've changed quite a bit since then," he said.
"I can say the same for you.... You remember Marie, don't you?" Rita said, smiling innocently at him.
He had to think a minute. "Marie Barone, sure. It's been a while."
Without warning Rita left them alone and they were at a loss for words. He had politely asked about her two years, how she liked it at Collegiate, and so on, but the conversation was strained and soon broke off. She was too self-conscious about her complexion.
Later Anne put on some records and a few people started dancing. Marie sat alone on the sofa watching Rita, attired in one of Miss Guzzo's slinkiest dresses and with her hair permed, dancing with a boy neither of them knew. A few of her old girlfriends came over to speak to her every so often, but she was too proud to mingle with them and they soon left her alone.
At one point in the evening she found herself dancing with Renzo because of a game Anne had devised. He held her stiffly and they went through the motions as the phonograph played a slow instrumental. Renzo was trying to spark a conversation. She couldn't even raise her eyes to him. His tone seemed overly polite, as if he were patronizing her. It occurred to her that he might be pitying her and she stiffened even more.
She didn't stay much longer. Leaving by the back, she didn't tell anyone she was going. She felt so miserable she wanted the earth to open up and swallow her right there. Further down the street she could see the fireworks display just above the backlot of the Marconi Hall. It was the end of Festa Day.
Somehow, she thought, if she could get through the next

few years of high school and still have some dignity, she'd be eternally grateful.

3

"Go! Go!" someone yelled from the stands.

Joey took the puck at his blueline and started up the right wing. At the corner of his eye he caught Tubby Minelli trying to catch up to him. Boofie was still in the defensive zone.

His Steelmaking teammates yelled to him from the bench. He only caught the blur of their red sweaters with the large S on the crest. He felt the surge of his blood quicken as he settled into his fluid stride. The puck cradled in his stick. His head held up. His eyes alert. His mind blank.

He saw that it was one-on-two against the Rail Mill defencemen.

At the other blueline he deeked toward the centre, drew the left defenceman in, and blew down the boards, hoping to cut in toward the net. His skates crunched hard into the ice. At the last second he turned to see where Tubby was. The other defenceman came bearing down on him. He forgot about passing the puck. There was just enough time to brace himself as the big guy took him and rammed him hard against the boards. The sticks went high and hit the glass. A shattering sound like an explosion echoed in the sparsely filled arena. Joey felt a sharp pain in his hip. His helmet scraped the glass. As he went down he felt the weight of the man on top of him.

Momentarily dazed he didn't realize the other man was deliberately pressing his elbow into his throat. The choking sensation reminded him of something. At the last minute he uncoiled his body violently and shoved the guy away.

Play was still going on. The defenceman, whom he only knew in passing, grinned coldly at him. The Rail Mill man must have been two inches over his own six-foot frame. He had a big nose and a nasty face.

"C'mon, Barone," he said, dropping his gloves, "we all know how chickenshit you are."

Joey was startled for a moment. The man was speaking as if he had a personal grudge against him. Or he had committed some offence against him. Then he realized he was being enticed into a fight because of his reputation. They knew he wouldn't fight for any reason in the Industrial League where fights were as frequent as games. And someone would as soon slash you over the arms as congratulate you on a good play.

It was his only way of maintaining some measure of dignity in playing in a third-rate league with a bunch of has-beens. But before he could skate away contemptuously, Tubby came barrelling in and tackled the defenceman from the side. Joey watched the proceedings with a curious detachment. It was hardly a contest. Tubby, much older and far out of shape, was no match for the larger man. In a few minutes the defenceman had Tubby's sweater over his head and was pummelling him with blows to the face and stomach. Joey could hear the muffled swearing and the yelps as the fists found their mark.

When the linesman finally pulled them apart the ice was splattered with blood. Tubby's face was a mess. Another tooth had been knocked out and blood was pouring freely from his mouth. At the sight of the blood the few fans started to scream and holler for more.

In a moment both benches had cleared and there was a brawl. Sticks and gloves were scattered over the ice. Men were earnestly beating away at one another. Some grappling on the ice. Others swinging away like mad. The referee and linesman stood at the boards, helpless, and shaking their heads. The fans were threatening to get out of control. Finally the arena's lights were shut off. The strains of the national anthem came through the sound system.

Later Tubby and another man had to be taken to the hospital for stitches. Steelmaking won the game, but they were all rather subdued in the dressing-room.

It was a small cement room with rubber mats on the floor and benches around the walls. Two old, rusty shower stalls were at the far end.

Donny Belsito passed him by shaking his head. "You call that hockey?" he scoffed.

Beansie, the tall gangling goalie, expressed his concern for Tubby. "Why does Tubby always get it like that?"

Tubby was a short rotund man who had small eyes and a raffish grin. He was happy-go-lucky enough ordinarily, but on the ice he was a raging maniac when he lost his temper. He had a chance to play semi-pro many years back with a team in central Michigan but hadn't lasted more than a year. Older and slower now, he was getting more than his share of beatings.

In the showers Joey saw the same beer bellies, the same thin legs and the hang-down-ass walk he was so used to seeing in the plant. Only instead of cleaning away the soot and grime, they were washing away the blood from the wounds of warfare. He could see their eyes shine as they never did in the plant. As they were dressing the mood picked up and someone yelled for the Vic.

Beansie spoke up instantly. "All right, but only for a few or my old lady'll nail me."

There were some wisecracks and horsing around as they picked up their smelly equipment and threw it into their bags. The air was a mixture of stale sweat and deodorant.

Joey looked at Donny and he agreed to go too. He didn't feel like going home just yet—not with Assunta acting so strangely ever since the funeral. Maybe he'd get so pissed he'd get rid of the sinking feeling in his stomach. His father's death had done something to him that he couldn't quite fathom. Something had ended and there was no going back.

Sitting beside the corpse of his father had affected him more than he had at first realized. A sort of indescribable fear had been lodged somewhere in his body and wouldn't soon go away.

When Donny finished dressing they walked up the stairs to ice level to watch the Sault Junior team practise for a while. Donny seemed pensive. The arena was empty except for a few people who had stayed to watch the practice. They went up to the first row of seats and watched silently.

Joey looked with concern at his friend. Donny had skated away from the brawl in disgust. Ordinarily that would have branded him as a coward. But Donny Belsito held a place of honour on the Steelmaking team. Besides being the oldest player in the league, he was the only one to have played professional in the NHL. And it was back in the late fifties when there had been only six teams and it was quite a measure of distinction.

Donny had also grown up in the West End and had been Joey's idol ever since he started playing hockey. Belsito had left a reputation at the McFadden rink as the best player to have come out of the neighbourhood. And there had been quite a few. He had been an inspiration to every kid who laced on a pair of skates. He had started his career at McFadden before he could barely tie his shoelaces, then had an illustrious career in the Sault's minor hockey program before going south to play Junior. That move more than anything else, Joey well knew, had ensured him a crack at the pros. And he had done it—played for the Detroit Red Wings for almost an entire season with the likes of Gordie Howe and Ted Lindsay. But a series of unfortunate injuries, coming too close upon each other, had toppled him from the pros. For a number of years afterward he "rode the buses," as he said, in the farm leagues till a third injury had ended his career completely. Doctors told him to hang up his skates. A few years later, however, he was playing in the Industrial League and working at the plant.

They had become good friends over the years. When Joey first joined the Steelmaking team he was too much in awe of Donny to say anything. But the fact that they played the same style of game—stressing speed and finesse—drew them together from the very start. In time Donny took Joey under his wing and set about teaching him the finer points of the game. The various land-training exercises to improve the skating muscles. How to shift and accelerate without losing stride. How to size up the weaknesses of defencemen. How to mentally prepare for a game. But, most important, Donny instilled in him a reverence for the game that went beyond ambition. That it didn't matter whether you played in the pros or in a kitchen-sink league, hockey was hockey, pure and simple—the only thing Canadians did the best in all the world. If you treated it well, it would do good things for you. If you abused it, somehow it would get back at you. And Donny had never expressed bitterness over his bad breaks.

"That's the way it goes," he'd say. "Maybe I couldda become one of the best. Maybe so. I had the moves. And I definitely had the desire. But maybe I couldda had my knees busted earlier in my career and never made the pros. At least I have that year. I ain't bitching. Hockey's been good to me. I love to play. They'll have to carry me out on a stretcher before I hang'em up."

And the way he was going Joey believed him. Donny was probably in better shape than most of the younger men in the league. He kept his body in fine trim by working out during the summers and playing ball. Short at 5′6″, he had a lean body without an ounce of fat on it. Although he had lost much of his speed he still had most of the quick reflexes that had been his trademark as a young man. He had been nicknamed The Cat way back for darting around defencemen and pouncing on the puck. His face, though, showed his true age. It was battered and scarred from many years in hockey. One of his eyebrows drooped. All his teeth were missing. And if that weren't enough, he had been hit badly on the side of the mouth with the blade of a stick, which caused him to smile crookedly.

Over the years Joey had also got to know Donny's family. His wife Nicole was a French girl whom he had known in the neighbourhood. His daughter Annalise was an artist and taught at a local high school.

Joey had to laugh recalling Annalise's peculiar habit of sitting high up in the corner seats with her sketchbook. She'd come to watch her father play occasionally and sketch hockey scenes when she was in high school. He knew her first as a bright girl who was determined to make her mark on the world. He used to listen to her speak about art, her face fluctuating between gloom and fervour. She wasn't sure how far her talent could take her. It was frightening. But maybe she had something special. She'd never know in any case unless she really tried it on her own. Joey enjoyed listening to her ambitions and encouraged her as much as he could. At that point she had been like a younger sister. But her fire and eagerness came to excite him beyond any brotherly concern. Later, when she was back for the summers from university, he had taken her out a few times. But she had developed an outward show of arrogance toward the city by that time. Her contempt seemed to take in all its occupants, including him.

"They're so blind here," she'd say. "Can't they see how ugliness pervades their lives? They sleepwalk through it all. It's so ghastly."

For some reason he had taken almost every remark against the city as a personal snub against him. He felt obliged to defend the ugliness, although he didn't know why. And she always questioned him. "How can you be so content here, Joey?" she'd say.

She had been the only girl he had really known—and that was mainly because she was Donny's daughter. She seemed to understand hockey. She genuinely listened to him and didn't make him feel too uncomfortable. In any case she had been living with hockey and its memories all her life. The first serious paintings she ever did were the hockey scenes from her sketches. It was so odd to see her up there sketching away while they were banging heads down below. Donny would always play his heart out if he knew his daughter was watching. And Joey couldn't deny that his own play took on a greater intensity if he knew Annalise's eyes were on him.

Yet her years away from home had changed her. She became more sure of herself—haughtier, in fact—and he could see she had made very different types of friends in Toronto. After university she had spent two years painting on her own, sending back desperate requests for funds that Donny always managed to meet without reservation. The two years had resulted in a lot of work done, but little success. There had been no exhibitions and very little recognition. Finally Donny had gone down in a van, packed her better canvases, and brought her back to the Sault. Joey hadn't seen much of her in those two years. He was shocked to see how badly her health had deteriorated. She had a stomach disorder and her skin had lost much of its colour. Yet the fire hadn't gone out of her eyes—and every so often she'd let him see that she wasn't beaten by a long shot.

In any case, she managed to get a job teaching art and she was back living with her parents. Joey had met her a few times for coffee, but he was rather quiet and unsure of himself in her presence. Every so often her fierce eyes, which had some kind of enchanting power, would look right through him. He had no idea of how to handle her. She was like some wild beautiful bird that had injured its wings.

Joey panned over the seats to the corner section where Annalise used to sit. He wondered what she was up to these days. Donny gave him a disgusted look and shook his head.

"After brawls like that I ask myself why I didn't quit a long time ago. It's fuckin' ridiculous. Are we playing hockey, or what?"

They looked at the Junior players going through their drills. Skating hard. Booming the pucks off the boards. With a serious sense of themselves. Young men with prospects.

He and Donny talked briefly about the year's crop of players: who was doing well and who hadn't lived up to expectations. They kept a close watch on the team and attended every home game at the Gardens. The old Sault arena was a squat low building, with a lighthouse tower at the front. It sat a little over 3000 and was a second home to him.

Upon arriving at the Vic they were surprised to find Tubby seated with the rest of the guys. His lips were swollen and discoloured. It was difficult for him to swill his beer. Exulting in the spotlight, he was bragging at length on how he'd get his revenge. The others, clearly sympathizing with his injury, were letting him have his hour.

He and Donny drew another table into the throng of men.

"Thanks for the help, Tub," Joey said quickly, knowing he had to make up to him.

There was a moment of silence. Tubby seemed to roll the remark over in his mind.

"Just pass the fuckin' puck next time, hotshot," he said, beaming.

Everyone laughed at the way the words came out. In a while an argument arose over hockey strategy. Joey had heard it so many times before that he was easily distracted by the people around him. He drank his beer slowly but steadily, knowing exactly how much he could put down without disturbing his rhythm after a game.

A bowling team with their sponsor's name on the back of their shirts was clustered in a far corner. In the middle was a high school basketball team, their crested jackets slung over the chairs. And right beside them was a group of middle-aged ladies with their curling sweaters still on. It was late enough that the conversation was loud and slurred.

He wasn't overly surprised to see some of the players from Rail Mill come in undetected and sit in a far corner of the tavern. Joey also spotted some good-looking girls sitting alone, drawing on their cigarettes like movie stars. But he was too shy to stare at them for long.

When the argument became heated he turned his attention back to the table.

"That's fuckin' right," Terry, the big millwright, raised his voice boisterously. "Beat'm in the alley, hey."

"Sure," Tubby said. "You see'm in the playoffs...the first game...trying to bust each other's heads in...to see who'll back down first...that's the only way."

Beansie, who was given to self-induced indignation with each glass of beer, said, "If youse guys didn't push 'em outta the crease I'd be up to my ears in bodies all the time. They'd take every inch unless you show 'em business."

"That's the way hockey is...."

"Sure," Beansie went on. "If the refs would let us play our way the Russians would have their asses whipped every time."

They were all very much aware that a Soviet team was going to be playing an exhibition game in the Sault that spring against the Junior team. Everyone was anxious to see the Russians after the famous series of 1972.

"Let me explain a few elementary propositions to youse guys," said Boofie.

"Ah, lay off, Boofie."

Boofie Pagnotta was the intellectual on the team. He was of average height with a boyish face that always seemed to be looking archly at you. He had won a hockey scholarship to Cornell in the early seventies, played only half a season, and had returned to the Sault because he was homesick. Joey had always found the derivation of his name odd. When Boofie first tried to explain he had played in Ithaca, New York, most of the guys on the team had scoffed that Buffalo was close enough. He was always trying to buffalo them anyway. So his name came to be Buffy. Then everyone kidded him about how full of hot air he was because of his smart-alecky remarks. The Italian for a puff of air was *buffo* and for a clown was *buffone*—so that eventually the "u" was spread out to Boofie.

"The Russians have what is called in most circles a sound

scientific method."

"Aw, fuck off."

"...of playing hockey. Our rough-hewn tactics do not deter them. In order to defeat them we all must read from the tactics of their real coach, a guy called Lenin."

"Yeah, Boofie, didn't he play for the Moscow Selects?" Terry said seriously.

"I'd rather say he played better at home than on the road."

"Aw, fuck off, Boofie," a few said in unison.

Beansie said, "All I can say to youse guys is that those bastards tonight weren't as cocky after the brawl. Hey, what can I tell youse." He shrugged his shoulders and laughed.

The others laughed at nothing in particular. Joey looked at Donny. He had been quiet, drinking his beer quickly. There was a scowl on his face that had gotten tighter with each remark from the guys.

Finally, in an imperious voice filled with contempt, he said, "Youse guys don't know the first thing about hockey."

The remark cut through the smug camaraderie and drew a storm of protest. Donny listened politely, his mood relaxing somewhat as he saw his words take effect.

"I repeat," he went on, "youse guys don't know what hockey is because you've never seen it and you've never played it."

"Whadda ya mean?" Tubby said.

"Hockey died in 1960," Donny said, sinking farther in his chair and looking abstractly at them.

"Not that again," Beansie said, snickering.

"Died in '60 when the Rocket retired—and buried in '67 with Expansion."

"C'mon...."

Donny shook his head, not the least annoyed by their disbelief. "Youse guys just won't see it. You're thick in the head—and you're young. Have you ever seen the Rocket play? Tell me, have you?"

"Yeah," Tubby said. "I seen'm on TV. So what?"

"So what, he says. It's like talking to stones. I played against him, that's so what! What d'ya see on TV? Only the bodies and the fuckin' beer commercials. You hadda see the fire in the Rocket's eyes. You hadda see'm carry two people on his back and his eyes flash at the goal. When he wanted to score nothing could stop'm. He didn't fuckin' shoot the puck into the corner and go after it like everybody does now. That's not fuckin' hockey. That's horseshit. You hadda see'm split the defence or go around on his backhand or get a pass and skate like a locomotive down his wing. You hadda try to stop him to know what hockey is. Hockey's dead here. Only the Russians come close to playing it like the Rocket. But they're fuckin' machines with ice in their veins."

They all were looking sheepishly at Donny. The words seemed to have some effect on them.

Beansie mentioned a few of the recent stars of the game.

"Sure, there're a few ghosts left who make the game interesting. But I tell ya that hockey died in '60."

Donny guzzled more beer. The words themselves seemed to have put him back into the fifties, face to face with the Rocket. His eyes were bright. His face flushed. Joey was instantly reminded of Annalise.

The others were clearly subdued by the passion in Donny's words. They looked uneasily around, embarrassed to catch each others' eyes. Finally, however, Beansie caught sight of the guys from Rail Mill and they quickly had an escape to more familiar emotions.

At that point Donny shook his head and motioned to Joey that it was time to leave. They both had day shifts the next morning. Besides, things looked to be getting mean again. Tubby's face had become dark and sinister.

Outside it had gotten colder. They walked toward their cars in silence. Joey watched his hot breath swoosh out, captivated by the way it danced out of sight. At Donny's car they stopped.

Joey said, "Did you really mean what you said about the

Rocket?"

"Damn right!"

"If hockey died why did you keep on playing then?"

"Because you wanna bring it back, that's why. You think it's still alive in you."

Joey paused to think about that. It couldn't be true. When things died they stayed dead. The neighbourhood. His father. His dreams. They had surely all ceased to exist. And now he knew how fragile everything else was. It was all paltry and insignificant by comparison. The membrane between being and not-being was so thin he could feel the cold wind blow through it and chill his spine.

Joey looked at Donny's scarred face under the dim light of the parking-lot. Tomorrow he would have to pick up his father's tools at Masonry.

"No," Joey protested. "I don't believe you. It's only memories."

"Maybe so," Donny said, opening the door and nodding his head unconvincingly. "Maybe so. I'm sorry about your father, Joey."

Joey just looked at him.

"You have to shake yourself out of it, that's all."

"It's not just him," Joey said, feeling the familiar choking sensation in his throat. "It's my mother too."

"You have to grow up a bit, kid. You have to do something with your life."

"Yeah...sure."

"Why don't you call Annalise some time. She's been asking about you. Or is she only a memory? Sometimes I don't know about you, kid."

It was late when he got home. The light in the TV room was on. He put the old Buick in the garage quietly, hoping at least that his mother would be asleep.

She was sitting in her usual place at the end of the sofa. With her legs tucked under her and her head back at an abnormal angle she seemed in a deep sleep. She gave out unhealthy wheezing and snoring sounds as if she were choking. The TV was playing an old gangster film. He recognized Richard Widmark. Victor Mature's forehead was a mass of frowns.

He looked closer at Assunta, trying to catch some semblance of himself in her. It wasn't in her coarse grey hair that she kept loose and straggly since the funeral. His was light brown and curled at the edges. Nor in the dark Italian face that was angular and wrinkled like a dried olive. His was fleshy and wide, with light skin that gave him hardly any beard. She was short and thin. He had grown almost a head above even his father. It was a wonder that he had issued from her at all.

Richard Widmark laughed coldly as he pumped two bullets into Victor Mature. The movie ended in a hail of gunfire and the sound of sirens.

Joey stepped toward the set as the national anthem played. Assunta gave a start and awoke.

"*Lasciale,*" she said groggily, as if she had been waiting to catch him.

"It's finished, Ma."

"Turn to the other channel," she said in Italian.

"Ma," he said in dialect, "it's been three weeks. You can't stay here all the time. Why don't you go to bed, uh."

"You go to bed," she snapped.

She hadn't slept in her bedroom since the funeral three weeks ago. The kewpie doll resting against the edge of the pillow hadn't been budged.

Instead, she had come to practically live on the sofa. There was a blanket and hot-water bottle close by. During the day she dozed off while watching TV in the position he had just found her in. At other times she slept fully reclined. She ate her meals off the end-table, read the *Grand Hotel* and sewed under the lamp. Most often, though, all she did was watch TV. At identical times each day, depending on his shift, she made him his meals, packed his lunch-pail, and did other assorted chores. The only time she left the house was to go to the seven o'clock Mass every morning. He did the grocery shopping and any other errands for her.

Her old friends had come regularly at the beginning to share her grief. They came one at a time and sat with her in the TV room with the set on. Assunta said a few kind words, but no more. Seeming to understand what was happening, they soon stopped coming altogether. Only the widow Angeline continued to visit.

The widow, whose full name was Bellini, was a stout woman in her early seventies, with untidy white hair and a gravelly voice. She and her husband Eugenio had emigrated well before the others from a village close to the Adriatic port of Pescara. Having lost her husband not much later, she had been forced to run a small family restaurant on James Street until her children had grown up. She had worked hard all her life and still had a mind of her own.

Once, he had asked her what was happening to his mother. It seemed Assunta would never snap out of it. Her behavior was starting to scare him.

"I've seen this happen before," the widow said. "One of my friends from the old country. Was married 40 years. Didn't know what to do when her husband died. Just sat around like a *melanzana* for weeks."

"But what can I do?" Joey pleaded.

"There's nothing anyone can do," she shrugged. "Be patient with her. Let her come out of it herself. It's still early yet. Maybe this is an old custom from her village. You don't know. Some of the old Italian women, what they do when their husbands pass away!" She raised her arms in disbelief. "It's too much. Maybe I'm lucky that Eugenio—bless his soul—went so young."

But the widow Angeline's words only went to increase his worry. He felt utterly helpless in his mother's presence. He had tried countless ways to get her to use the regular bed, all to no avail. Even to use Marie's empty bed upstairs, if she was squeamish about her own. But Assunta had only stared at him as if he were dense.

He had even been on the phone to Marie constantly since the funeral. All she did, however, was try to reassure him that it was temporary.

"But it's getting worse," he said the last time, only a few days ago. "I'm getting scared, Marie. Really scared."

"Maybe she's doing this just to punish us," Marie said, her voice cold and analytical.

"C'mon, are you crazy? What for?"

"For what she overheard the day of the funeral. For the way we've turned away from her. It could be anything. I wouldn't put it past her."

"You're crazy—you should see her."

"She'll be all right. Don't worry so much. I think deep down she's indestructible, no matter how much she's whined about her ailments."

Joey changed his tone of voice.

"Marie, you've got to do something and help me."

He had to speak softly, even though he was using the basement phone. These conversations with Marie always seemed furtive. If he wasn't self-conscious about his mother overhearing, he was afraid she'd pick up the phone upstairs and listen in.

Marie had asked him to wait until the end of the school term in June. She'd come up for the summer and see if anything could be worked out. She'd even see if there were any jobs open in the Sault in the interim. Toronto was becoming intolerable. She didn't like the idea of raising Michael alone.

"In the meantime," she said, "try to speak to her. Try to teach her some English."

But as Joey looked at the impassive face of his mother he knew that speaking to her was as difficult a thing as he could do.

Even now he had trouble saying the obvious in his terrible

dialetto.

"Ma, close the TV before you fall asleep, okay. It's not good."

"*Sí, sí,* go to sleep, Joey. *Sei un buon ragazzo*—you're a good boy."

In bed that night he had his familiar dream of skating on a limitless expanse of a lake as huge as Superior. He thought it was a lake because it was so huge and he was alone with only the sky above him. He was skating slowly against a light cold breeze, keeping the puck ahead of him in regular pit-pats of his hockey stick. His hockey uniform felt snug and protective on him, although the sweater wasn't the familiar colour of any of his previous teams. There seemed to be no hurry to get anywhere. Only the secure feeling that he was protected against the cold and he was moving in hard sure strides against the Northern expanse. He felt invincible, and the odd colouring of his sweater seemed to substantiate this. The dazzling white light, which issued from under the ice, made the translucent surface glow with incredible beauty.

4

From his position in the ceiling crane Joey slowly manoeuvred the pot over the last ingot mould. The pot held 270 tons of liquid steel. Gigantic hooks the size of a sidewalk held the pot secure just a few feet from the top. Boofie, dressed in a silver asbestos suit on the ledge below, removed the stopper and the liquid steel streamed into the mould. White smoke immediately billowed up past the crane. As the white heat rose in the mould thousands of sparks jumped out like tracer bullets for yards around. The light from the molten steel was so intense no-one could look at it without dark glasses. Soon the mould was filled. They stood on rail tops in the pit like a chain of miniature volcanos, their tops glowing with white heat.

After the stopper was put back in place Joey inched the pot gently to the bottom of the pit area where it could be cooled. It was the end of his shift. The ingots would later be stripped and brought to the Mould Yards to cool. After they were re-heated in the soaking pits they were finally brought to the various rolling mills to be shaped.

He waited inside the crane for his relief. Even though the tap was over, it was still too noisy to take a nap. Besides, too many General Foremen were around during the day shift. He reached under the seat and picked up a battered copy of *Playboy.* Down below he saw Boofie and the men heading for the change-room.

This was the best part of the shift. He could look forward to a nice hot shower and walking toward the punch-out clock. Not that he detested his job. It just seemed he was perpetually waiting. If it wasn't for the end of his shift, it was for his relief, or for the end of a tap. He could do his job blind-folded. He often felt that he was half asleep inside the dark mills with their sulphurous smoke and incessant noise.

His father had tried on a few occasions to get him to apply for various apprenticeships in the plant trades.

"You're not a kid anymore," Adamo had said. "You got to find a trade you like doing. When people hear my name, what do they think? 'He's a bricklayer.' When they hear your name, what do they think, hey?"

A failure, Joey thought. He didn't care to improve his station. He had never felt himself a steelplant worker. It was only a temporary state of affairs. Ever since losing out in hockey he had been waiting for things to end, not to happen. He had turned inward, felt himself diminished. He was thus prone to a life of memories, introspection, and dreams, which was foreign to him. It was as if time had been held suspended since he was eighteen. Only when he played hockey did he feel alive as before. Hockey seemed to empty him inside. There was no innerness. He was no more and no less than what he did.

For once Beansie came earlier than expected. He whistled up to him and Joey came down the ladder. There was a gash in Beansie's lip. He was smiling from ear to ear. Joey knew him to live in a decrepit house with a junkyard in the back and autographed pictures of Roy Rogers and Dale Evans on his kitchen wall.

"Didja hear?" Beansie said, all excited.

"What?"

"What happened at the Vic last night?"

"No." He was anxious to leave.

Beansie gave him the story as fast as he could. The brawl at the rink had been resumed in the Vic parking-lot. Tubby and a few others had gotten their revenge on the Rail Mill guys. Beansie was prouder than punch. He had gotten a few good licks in before someone had cut open his lip. Everyone got away before the police arrived. Joey left him chortling as he climbed up to the crane.

Up in the change-room everyone was talking about the game and the fights. They were all laughing and swearing.

"Hey, Joey," someone yelled at him, "didja hear?"

As he was passing the large circular basin where some of the old timers were washing their faces and armpits, a toothless old man with a white hairy chest spotted him.

"Youse guys played like fuckin' bums last night, Joey."

"Yeah," someone else laughed. "You had so much lead in your pants I thought you'd be shitting pencils."

Joey grinned good-naturedly. He could hear the raised voices of a few other men in the aisles talking about all the fights.

When he got to his locker he found Donny already undressed and ready for the shower.

"Hear what happened?" Joey said.

"Yeah, only the bullshit. Everyone has his own story to

tell."

"What can you expect?" he shrugged.

"Someone's got to change the rules or the league will fold. Nobody's really interested in playing anymore. All they want to do is beat each other's brains in."

Joey put his hardhat away and started taking off his smelly clothes. They hadn't been washed in weeks.

"If the league folds, then what?" he said with concern. "Where can we play?"

Donny took some time before answering. Casually he said, "I've been thinking a lot since last night. Maybe it's time I hung up the skates anyway."

It was said so matter-of-factly that Joey didn't know how to take it. There was an uneasy silence.

"My union work is starting to occupy more of my time," Donny went on. "And Nicole's always been nagging me about injuries."

Joey didn't speak. Donny was a union steward and expected to go up for the executive of the local soon.

"Well," Donny said, his tone apologetic and unnatural, "you can't keep playing all the time. Even the Rocket had to retire."

Joey remained silent as they went to the shower-room. He was afraid to look Donny in the eye. It had been a tough season so far, what with the brawls, and his friend was probably in a bad frame of mind.

The room smelled of wet greasy socks. Joey went under the nozzle and tried to wash away the cobwebs of his shift. Donny quickly spread a thick coat of lather over his body.

"Annalise was at the game last night and saw everything," Donny raised his voice above the sound of the spray.

"Yeah?" Joey said, recalling with regret that he had played a bad game.

"She really let me have it when I got home. She was waiting up for me and all. Said that we were a bunch of stupid kids fighting like that. That it looked so ridiculous from the stands. That I was much too old for that sort of thing. She said I was old enough to be a grandfather, as a matter of fact. If only I were, I told her. But she really made me see what I've been putting off too long now. It's a kid's game, Joey, pure and simple. I don't know why I've played so long."

Back at their lockers Donny asked him to wait for him—they'd walk together to the gate.

Joey shook his head. "I got to do something."

"What's that?"

"Empty out the old man's locker at Masonry."

The Department had sent him a note. He had to do it now or they would confiscate the contents. He had put it off too long already.

On his way to the Masonry change-room he thought about what Donny had told him. Everything had to end, he supposed. The image of his emaciated father came to mind: "Joey, what's going to happen to my tools?"

The change-room was a two-storey brick building separated from the mills just off the main road to the gate. Joey timed it so he'd get there after the shift change. There were only a few stragglers left. He headed straight for the locker. Putting his lunchpail on the bench, he looked at the door for a minute.

When he was a kid he had always avoided touching his father's personal stuff. Most of the items came from the old country. Adamo made sure he was constantly supplied with such things as heavy cotton undershirts, aftershave cream, and brilliantine. These things were from a different world, one that Joey felt he had no right to touch.

As he opened the locker it occurred to him that only because Adamo was dead did he have a right to break into his private world.

It was all there, exactly as his father had left it after his last shift. Dust had settled over everything.

Adamo's shaving utensils were neatly arranged on the top shelf. There was a mug with dry hardened lather, a brush, a straight-blade razor, and a small mirror. Each piece appeared to have been used for decades. Joey knew his father had never been given to trying new-fangled things. Once something served him well he'd use it till it was completely worn.

It brought to mind how his father had kept the first used car he ever bought—a black '49 Chevrolet—all the way up to the late sixties. After having been driven to school a few times Joey refused any more rides.

"Whattsa matter?" Adamo asked him.

"Why don't you get a new car, Babbo," he said defiantly.

"Whattsa matter with this one?"

"Nobody has a car like that anymore. The kids at school laugh at me."

"It still runs good, right. When a machine runs good, you don't change it do you—just because it looks old?"

"Aw, Babbo, you know what I mean. That car belongs in the scrap heap."

"And when your parents are old—do you put them in the scrap heap?" he had said, his face burning with anger.

A light green hardhat, the unmistakable badge of a bricklayer, rested to the right. His father's workclothes—green pants and a few shirts heavily stained with mortar—hung down one of the sides. An apron with the mason's tools was slung down the other. There was the brick hammer with one pointed end to cut brick. And the various trowels to spread the mortar and cement. Along with the zig-zag rule, the square, the plumb and line, and a couple of chisels. Having worked as a Helper in Masonry during his student days, when his father had first gotten him into the plant, Joey knew how the various tools were used. He had seen expert bricklayers cut, trim, and lay bricks with quick, sure movements that somehow became one fluid motion to the eye. He had also helped Adamo enough times around the house to be interested at one time in taking up the trade.

Adamo used to say, "It's as honest and good work as you'll find. To build things that last when you die. To feel the brick in your hands—these pieces and blocks that make larger things than you are. But not in the plant, Joey. That's no place for a real bricklayer. You have to build houses or churches or bridges—that's what you have to build."

At the bottom of the locker, along with some other tools and used clothes, was an old misshapen pair of work boots, with the extra reinforcement flaps over the upper arches. They were coated with grime and mortar.

He looked closer at the boots, trying to picture his father walking through the dark mills in that slow open gait of his that looked so much like a penguin's waddle. A bricklayer going to the various furnaces to line them with fire-brick. Keeping the inferno going. Instead of building homes and bridges as he had always meant to.

Joey took out a trowel, turning the handle delicately in his hand. The grain of wood had been smoothed down by such long use that it fit the contours of the palm perfectly. He moved his fingers over the smooth texture, feeling for any mark or slight depression in the wood. There was no telling how long his father had used the trowel. It could have been the first one he had ever owned since his apprenticeship days in Italy.

It felt good to handle the tool. To turn it over. To feel its perfect balance. To clean off the mortar and feel the cool dusty smoothness of the steel spade.

But at that moment a strange feeling overcame him. It swept over him like the cold wind of his dream. It was diffused and vague and he wasn't exactly sure what it meant. But it had to do with his father's life. And his father's death. Death levelled a man to nothingness. And therefore his life wasn't really his own. There was some larger pattern in which it fitted. He could only realize himself within this pattern, over which he had no control. It wasn't exactly to his father that his life belonged, but to something having to do with his father. The tools, somehow, made him feel it in his bones.

When the sensation passed he was left confused. Handling

the other tools, he tried to regain the feeling that had swept away his self-doubt. But it was no use. It wouldn't come back. Yet each trowel, like the first, fit so well in his palm that they could have been made for him.

Joey placed all the tools on the bench for a minute and took a long look at them. It was almost as if his father had left a part of himself behind, he thought.

"Babbo?" he said without thought.

Presently, some people came in. He felt embarrassed and strange. Quickly he stuffed all the tools and old clothes into a garbage bag. As he was closing the door, however, he noticed he had overlooked some photographs stuck at the top corners.

Extremely old, they were rounded at the edges and yellowed by age. One was unmistakably his mother as a very young woman standing beside a tree, with a fallow field in the background. She seemed no more than nineteen or twenty. Her dark, slightly curly hair came down to her shoulders. Wearing a simple cotton dress adorned with flowers, she was smiling plaintively at the camera.

Her extreme thinness and the particular angularity of her face made him immediately think of Marie. The old photograph couldn't completely hide her attractive features. Joey had to look closely to confirm his initial impression. Somehow, probably because Assunta had been a mail-order bride, he had never thought of her as being attractive.

The other two were baby pictures he had never seen before of himself and Marie. With his light hair, he was sitting on a flat-seated tricycle learning to walk by pushing forward. He looked chubby and healthy. Marie was standing beside the old wooden fence of their garden, holding what looked like a bicycle bell and looking rather forlornly at the camera.

Joey was struck by the thought of his father seeing those pictures every time he dressed for work.

Without thought he quickly took them down and put them in with his tools.

5

It was late in February when she finally received the letter. Her mother had left it with the rest of the mail on the kitchen table. It had been conspicuously placed to the side, as if it had been studied for a while and then haphazardly tossed back.

Marie's heart started to beat furiously. Without removing her coat or boots she stared at it for a minute, trying to prepare herself for the worst. After all, it wasn't as if her whole life depended on it.

She tore open the letter.

Dear Miss Barone,
We are pleased to inform you that you have been unconditionally accepted by the University....

For a while she couldn't quite believe what the words were saying. Then a warm delicious glow started to collect in her stomach, sprang up suddenly, and burst in her head, causing her scalp to tingle.

At that moment, however, she heard the sounds of her mother making dinner downstairs. Instead of bringing her boots and coat to the basement closet, she left them just inside the back door, took her books, and quickly went up to her room.

She sat on the bed and for the next fifteen minutes read and reread the letter, savouring every last morsel of triumph. Presently, tears sprang to her eyes. Marie watched them plop onto the paper, interested in seeing which of the words would be hit.

It was utterly quiet in her room. She raised her head and looked at what had virtually been her home the past four years. There was space for only a dresser, a bed, and a desk. It was a refuge she could call her own, yes, but it was also the last corner she had been backed into. It seemed so small at times that she was afraid to breathe too hard lest she suffocate.

Ever since Adamo had built the second bathroom in the basement, her parents rarely came upstairs to the second floor. She had the duty of keeping her room and Joey's tidy and of making the beds. Some days the only time she'd see them was at dinner—or if she relaxed in front of the TV.

Marie thought of herself as a foreigner in her own house. Usually it was home from school, rest for a while before doing the beds, the sullen dinner, dishes, homework, and perhaps a little TV before going to bed. If neighbourhood friends arrived to see her parents, she'd immediately go up to her room and close the door, not even bothering to say hello. Her radio, if turned on loud enough, just managed to drown out the exuberant and sickening Italian voices.

As for the neighbourhood, it was crumbling all around her. At least she could say she had prevailed there. People were moving out steadily, either because of expropriation or to avoid further depreciation on their property. Since the erection of the International bridge, the future of James Street had long been determined. Most of the stores were vacant now and ready for demolition. She had heard her father speaking to his friends occasionally of how business owners were losing money. Adamo knew Pee-Pee quite well, and he had done some masonry work for Spina, the owner of the hardware store.

"The kids, they move out first," Adamo said. "As soon as they get enough money to buy a house in the East End. They move away from their parents. They don't want to do with their parents anymore, hey. They become *English,*" and he'd make an insulting Italian gesture with his hands. "And Spina told me—he said people stopped coming from the old country. *Porca miseria,* what're you going to do? It's all finished. Things that you build, they have to be torn down. Look how many years I work on this house. I ask for a good price, let me tell you. They don't take *my* house so easy."

Ghost town or not, however, she couldn't stand it anymore. As she walked home from school, the very sight of the familiar buildings and the derelict houses was repugnant. It was as if she were walking back in time, while she was so anxious to burst out of her old skin and emerge totally new. She had something of a chance to spread out her wings at school, but when she went back home it was the same old thing. She crept around like a bug.

The only feasible way to salvage some measure of self-respect in all this was to stay in her room as much as possible —stay there and wait.

Now the waiting had paid off. She could almost taste her freedom. Giving out a whoop of joy, she raised her arms in triumph and fell back onto the bed, unable to control a fit of delirious laughter.

Later she went downstairs and phoned Rita from the TV room. Rita's parents had long since moved from the West End to a fashionable house in a new development in the expanding north end of the city. She had just been accepted by the new local university. It was a single brick building that once was the Christian church on the Indian reservation. Rita was quite content to stay in the city. She had a steady boyfriend and was thinking of settling down in the near future. When Marie spoke to her about the more ambitious possibilities that life had to offer, Rita merely crinkled her face in exaggerated helplessness and said, "For me a home and kids. That's all I want. You can have the rest."

Rita asked her if she had told her parents yet.

"My mother knows I got the letter, but she doesn't know what's inside. I can't wait till I break the news. First her, tonight. Then my father."

"Be careful with them, Marie," Rita warned.

As it turned out, maybe from her experience in having to serve them at Guzzo's, Rita had developed an easy manner with older people. It was interpreted by Assunta as the exemplary behavior of a good Italian daughter. Her friend had the knack of indulging them in their customs, and at the same time of being above it all. She'd often walk arm-in-arm with her mother downtown. Or she'd talk endlessly of children and recipes with the neighbourhood women on their front steps. Later she could easily laugh about it.

"What's the harm," she'd say. "People are funny. They just want to feel a little comfortable with you. They don't want to feel that you threaten them. Is that so hard? Let me tell you, Marie, it hasn't been too easy for our people."

Marie couldn't say she envied Rita her easy-going manner. It was probably the one ingredient that had extended their friendship so long. Rita was very accommodating and good-natured. She was able to offset her moodiness and aloofness.

"I will," Marie said. "But they can't stop me now."

"Marie, why do you fight so much? You always fight. Has it ever occurred to you that maybe no-one's fighting back?"

Marie laughed it off. They agreed to meet later in the evening for coffee. When Joey came in, Marie followed him down to dinner.

The table was set for three. Adamo was working afternoons. Assunta was at the stove, her back to them. The way she was sullenly absorbed in her work indicated that something was amiss. Marie looked at her closely, observing how she avoided her eyes. And when she spoke she only said a few words to Joey.

It was virtually impossible to speak to her mother these days. Marie had found that her Italian had deteriorated to the point where she got stuck fairly often. It was so frustrating at times that she had to avoid saying anything but the most habitual phrases. If she used English equivalents Assunta would get annoyed and refuse to understand. Marie found herself speaking like a child, regressing ever more into the only infantile expressions that came to mind.

Complaining about this to her father once, she was surprised by the vehemence of his reply.

"Why don't you learn Italian at your high school, *stupida!*"

It hadn't even occurred to her to take Italian. She needed

all the math and science courses in order to enter a math program at university. She had, surprisingly, found herself to be very adept in mathematics, often scoring perfect marks on tests and exams. She liked the step-by-step method of solving problems and the indisputable nature of the results. She was one of the few girls in the city who had done well in the provincial math aptitude tests.

"But Babbo," she said, shaken by the reply, "it's up to her to learn English. This is an English-speaking country."

Her father looked at her in such a knowing, sad way that she entertained the possibility that he might know more than she thought.

"And this is an Italian-speaking house," he said.

She and Joey started eating while her mother was still preparing the salad. The silence stretched. Joey kept his face close to the huge plate of gnocchi, obviously sensing something was wrong.

"*Per la Madonna di Dio, Giuseppino,* lift your face," her mother said in dialect. "You eat like a horse, you be a horse."

Joey made a face, as if he had heard the adage hundreds of times. He had a voracious appetite. His two preoccupations, sports and watching TV, pretty well kept him out of her hair, but he could be a pest at times. Marie at one time had felt it incumbent upon her to try to counteract the influence of their parents by attempting to rear him according to certain principles she had picked up away from home. But Joey had become obstinate as he grew older and had ended up doing the exact opposite of what she told him.

"He is a horse," Marie said playfully.

"What a farmer!" Joey made a face at her.

"My dear, what rudeness at the dinner table."

Her mother looked sternly at him. "Joey, you eat slower. You make yourself sick. Then I have to take care of you."

"Ah, we have a game at seven. I gotta go."

"*Basta,* Joey."

"Ah, Ma...."

"You eat slower," she raised her voice.

He made a feeble effort to eat like a regular human being, but once she wasn't looking he started wolfing down his food again. His bag and stick were at the bottom of the stairs, ready to go.

Marie looked at her mother. "Ma, the letter—you see it?"

"Joey, eat some vegetables now," Assunta disregarded her. "You never eat enough vegetables."

"Ma, you see the letter?"

"I see it."

Her mother looked anxiously at her for a moment, in an expression of such doleful consequence that Marie had to lower her eyes from embarrassment.

Later, when Joey was finished, Assunta put another piece of chicken onto his plate. "You eat that, Joey. *Non hai mangiato 'bastanza.*"

"Ma," Marie tried to intercede for him, "already he eat three ..." and she couldn't find the word for "pieces".

"He didn't eat enough," her mother looked at him, as if it were a personal insult against her. "Joey, eat that. I don't want you to eat in front of the TV tonight."

"Ma, can I have some pop?" Joey said.

"Maria, get some pop in the cantina."

Joey left shortly after. Marie started piling the dishes. Assunta was still eating. She always started late and lingered over her food. It was a source of continuous puzzlement that while her mother forced the food down their throats she herself ate sparingly and remained amazingly thin.

"Ma, I'm going to Toronto," Marie said abruptly. "They..." She couldn't find the Italian word for "accepted". "They took me."

There was a pause.

"Ma?"

"Speak to your father," Assunta snapped back. "Why do you bother me?"

"Ma, I have to go. More times I go to school, better job."

"You tell to your father."

Marie was burning to explain. There were so many things to say, such exciting possibilities to share—and here she was unable to render them in their simplicity to her own mother. She could just as well have been speaking to a stone.

"Ma, I wanna tell you," she pleaded.

"These things, I don't understand," Assunta said, as if it were an acknowledgement of defeat. And then in a more irritable tone: "You go to school—good. You smart—good. But you crazy. Your head in the clouds. The older you get, the crazier you get. I don't understand you. To *Toronto* you want to go?"

"Most people, the parents, they would be happy for this. But you...you..." and she couldn't find any Italian words whatsoever. She stopped. She could feel herself breathing heavily. Her hands were soaked in dishwater.

"You go to school here like Rita. What's the matter with that?"

"This place here, Ma, it's not such a good school. I wanna go to one of the best schools. Understand? It's important to me."

"Yeah, you become doctor," she said sarcastically.

Marie raised her voice. "Maybe I will."

"*Ma,* yeah."

"Yes! What do you know, ah, Ma? You speak to my teachers? You read the books I read? You do the things I do? You don't even know me."

Assunta gave a short biting laugh. "I don't know you? Why, *carina,* I wash the shit from your pants all the time."

Her mother's earthy vulgarity never ceased to sting her. She would always manage to find something to use against her, something that would strike at the bone and belittle her beyond measure. As a girl, whenever she was particularly naughty or Assunta found fault with her, her mother would maliciously bring up the fact that she wet her bed well past the acceptable age. "*Che stupida ragazza,* you pissed your pants like a fountain," she'd say. Or, "I had to wash your sheets every day, you little pisser." Even when other people were present: "Look at her, the little piss-pants of the street." It seemed her mother took delight in turning the knife brutally and humiliating her.

In the silence Marie could feel her indignation rising into a sharp, searing hatred.

"I'll do my own clothes," she said in English, glancing over her shoulder at her mother's implacable shape.

Assunta turned slightly. Marie caught the blank questioning face. It seemed to waver momentarily, as if unsure of how to proceed. Or as if it had gone too far.

Marie continued in English, her tone as icy and vindictive as she could make it.

"What's the difference if I speak English or Italian to you? You don't understand either way. I don't care anymore. If you want to know me learn my language. That's all there is to it. And I'm going as far from here as I can get. You can go back to where you came from, for all I care."

Marie wasn't sure how much her mother had picked up. Sometimes she pretended she understood less than she actually did.

"Speak Italian, *pazza*."

"If I want to speak English I'll speak English."

Assunta shrugged her shoulders wearily and turned back to her food.

Finishing the dishes Marie wiped her hands. She stood at the head of the table, looking down on her mother.

"Ma, I *have* to go away," she said in Italian, trying to make her understand.

"I do the best for you, Marietta."

There seemed no answer to that. She turned her head away, trying to control the emotion that was damming up her thoughts.

But Assunta's tone became sour again: "I cook your food. I wash your clothes. I clean up your mess. And then what do you want to do? You want to leave. You can't even take care of yourself. Is this gratitude?"

"Gratitude!" she said, shaking her head incredulously. "*È mia vita,* Ma. It's my life you're speaking about."

"*Ma,* sure...."

"You can't stop me," Marie said coldly.

"Do what you want. You don't listen anymore. You read your books. They teach you how to act? You too good for this family?"

"There's more in the world, Ma, than cooking and keeping house for a man. You don't understand. A girl has to make a life for herself. There are no dowry trunks here. You still live in the old country. You don't understand anything about this place."

"*Ma,* sure...." she turned her head away disgustedly.

"Many of the students, they go away to school."

"But not Rita, ah. She's a good daughter."

She couldn't understand her mother's reasoning. She pulled out a chair and sat down at the table, wanting to understand what she was saying. It seemed that Assunta wasn't telling her everything.

"Is it because you think I won't come back? Or is it because I'm a girl, Ma? Is that why you don't want me to go?"

Her mother looked blankly at her, as if she had missed the point entirely.

"Can't you tell me?" Marie said.

Assunta merely made a wry face. She got up and brought her plate to the sink, obviously annoyed.

"I don't want to speak anymore. You speak to your father."

"But, Ma, you don't talk anything. I don't know about you. You don't tell me things. I can't tell you things."

Marie was choked with emotion, ready to cry at any second.

But Assunta reacted angrily. "You go away then! I don't care!"

She stiffened instantly. "I will! I will! See if I don't!"

"And see if I care if you never come back!"

"I won't! I hate this place. I won't come back, don't worry about that."

Marie's whole body was bristling with anger.

Her mother shouted: "You're nothing but an *ingrata* who can't even wipe herself clean in the ass. See what you do!"

"And you, Ma—what about you?" Marie yelled back, wanting to hurt. "You couldn't even get married by yourself. Did Babbo choose you from a book? Did your parents sell you like a sack of potatoes?"

Assunta slapped her hard across the face. Stepping back, Marie was absolutely thunderstruck. It was the first time she had been hit since she was a girl. Putting her hand to her cheek, she felt such a tide of emotion rising up in her throat that she was rendered speechless. One instant she felt the urge to break down and sob. To hug her mother fiercely and ask for her forgiveness. The next she was loathing her with an unrestrained passion.

They stared at one another, both as surprised and helpless as they could be. Her mother's face then assumed such a terribly pained expression that Marie again felt an overwhelming desire to go into her arms. But, somehow, a more powerful force kept her back. Neither of them made a move toward the other.

The next moment Marie found herself running upstairs, unable to control her tears. She quickly put on her coat and boots and left the house. Walking down the street, the cold freezing her tears, she was overtaken by a blinding hatred of her mother. Of her ignorant peasant ways and her stupid dialect. Of her screaming. And her abominable eating habits. Her cheap hairspray and the way she had her hair done. Her stupid obsession with food. The way she made them all eat until they were bursting. And the way she repeated things so often, not even listening to what was said to her. She was so stuck in her ways. So unchangeable. And so cold. Like a stone.

So help her, she'd never speak to her again. She'd show her she could do things on her own. Go away to school and never see her again. She'd show her.

Later that evening she met Rita downtown at a coffee shop and told her everything that happened.

"Maybe you shouldn't have said those things," Rita said.

"You don't know how much I hate her."

"But Marie..."

"She's never loved me. She hasn't shown me the slightest bit of affection even. Only finding fault with me. Telling me this and that all the time. Treating me like a little girl all the time. Never encouraging me. She knows nothing about me. She's never even tried, Rita. She deserves it. It's as if I've been entirely alone in that house. I'll never speak to her again, so help me."

Luckily, when she got home that night Assunta wasn't there. Joey was watching TV.

For some reason Marie went straight to her parents' bedroom and sat on the bed. Staring at herself in the dresser mirror, she noticed her eyes were still a little discoloured. Even though her acne had not completely cleared, she had to conclude her face wasn't that bad to look at. She had tried to experiment with makeup on a few occasions, according to the information she received from women's magazines. It hadn't turned out all that bad, actually, but it all seemed futile as long as her body remained plump and unattractive. It had been her experience that male eyes never stayed fixed to a girl's face too long.

It sometimes seemed to her that her high-school years had gone by in one long embittering nightmare. In all that time only one boy had taken an interest in her. And it was another Renzo Lepera experience. He was a thin boy with thick glasses and a pinkish face whom the others called Booby—a nickname that was more than deserved. Unlike Renzo, however, he hadn't been transformed, and she had to persistently repel his bungling advances through a whole school year. The boys she had really been interested in had never given her a second glance. It was as if it had been a test and they had failed to discern her other body underneath the cocoon. She had given them no hints either. They had to find out for themselves. And it was humiliating to be so clearly snubbed. She took it as a personal affront.

Who needed boys anyway, she thought, if they expected you to be a giggling Kewpie doll? She was too serious about maintaining her high grades and getting out of the West End to fool around like some of the other girls.

"But it's not only because you're studious," Rita had once told her. "You're so glum all the time. Who wants to go out with a stick-in-the-mud? Why can't you smile and enjoy life a little?"

How could she, though, when it was all such a vicious circle? Surely someone had to love her first, she thought. Someone had to see through the surface and open her up.

Marie couldn't help thinking of her body as gross and indecent. Its urges caused her constant embarrassment and revulsion. Every so often it was overcome by a sort of befuddling daze that seemed to paralyze her mind. All sensation was focused in between her legs. Her blood felt viscous and heavy. She had vivid disquieting dreams of faceless men breathing down on her, causing goose bumps all over her body. A while back she had seen a movie of a couple of men, unwashed and unkempt in Cinemascope, contemptuously manhandling a rather arrogant woman before raping her. The scene had such a disarming effect on her that she had orgasmed in her seat. It was so unexpected and so scary that she didn't go to films for a few months afterward. But variations of the scene had crept into her dreams. She'd wake up wet between the legs the next morning.

It seemed if she wasn't wetting the bed one way she was doing it another. It was so debasing. She couldn't talk about these things even to Rita.

There was absolutely no-one to talk to.

Sometimes she just couldn't help it and did the unpardonable—touched herself to relieve that intense befuddlement that consumed her body like a fever. And these things just couldn't be related to Father Sarlo in the confessional. She'd be shamed beyond measure if he ever recognized her voice. It also stopped her from going to church altogether. She felt too unclean to be in the presence of statues with beatific expressions on their faces. Or with holy water and incense. And Father Sarlo's admonishing wrath for all the sinful.

She had long ago stopped fooling herself that she could control the urges of her body. It had wiped out her religion altogether and therefore the last thing she had in common with her mother. Her refusal to go to church anymore had caused so much friction between them that this day's open breach was long in coming.

It was enough to make her obliterate the past five years. Put them away in some dark compartment of her memory where they'd never be opened. And start fresh somewhere else. Away from a dead neighbourhood in a narrow-minded provincial city. Away from a family that had nothing in common with her—and a mother who lived in another world.

Out of habit Marie searched for the key to the Hope Chest. The overcoat pockets in the closet. Under the bed. The dresser where her mother kept all sorts of things like an inveterate hoarder. Old bank books and furniture bills. Sales slips. Broken watches and jewellery. Commemorative photos of deceased people. A few of herself and Joey at their first communion and confirmation. Old stamps from Italy. And all manner of small trinkets and odd bric-a-brac she had collected in the past fifteen years. But nothing before Assunta had come over from Italy.

The good jewellery was kept in an opened shoebox in the top drawer. Pearls and necklaces. Earrings. A couple of old rings. All revoltingly cheap stuff her mother had bought from the five-and-dime stores. When Marie was a kid she used to go with Assunta to Kresge's and Woolworth's and see her be absolutely fascinated by all the bright displays of merchandise.

On the other side of the top drawer were the handkerchiefs and smaller apparel like scarves and gloves. She pressed her hands over everything quickly to make sure nothing was hidden inside. The sight of her mother's personal things was vaguely repulsive, as if they brought her presence closer than she cared to have it. Indeed, every so often she looked up to make sure Assunta had not come upon her unawares. She thought she'd die if she ever caught her.

The next drawer had lingerie and *mutande,* which was the only name Marie used for panties. She went through the drawer very quickly. She was becoming increasingly revolted by the whole exercise. The mere sight of her mother's handmade *mutande,* made of plain coarse cotton, made her stomach queasy. They were the same kind Assunta had made for her till she absolutely refused to wear them when she was fourteen.

Marie went through everything else too quickly to care anymore. Her interest had evaporated. She thought of the possibility of breaking the trunk open with a crowbar. But the whole point, upon closer deliberation, was that she wanted to see what was inside without her mother knowing.

But it was getting late. Her mother was sure to return at any minute. Fear of being caught completely snuffed out any remaining curiosity.

All the lights were out and she was in bed later that night when she heard the slow footsteps of her mother ascending the stairs. Assunta used to check up on them when they were younger, but she had stopped a while back.

It occurred to her that Assunta might have discovered something askew in her bedroom and was coming up to question her. Or perhaps she was sorry for having struck her and was coming to ask her forgiveness. Either way, however, Marie dreaded seeing her. Assunta was the last person in the world she wanted comfort from at this moment.

She'd show her.

Assunta seemed to tiptoe to the door. Marie closed her eyes and pretended to be asleep. The door opened slightly. She felt the light from the hallway. She determined to pretend to be asleep no matter what.

There was a long pause. Marie hoped with all her might that her mother would go away and leave her alone. She wanted no part of her. She would show her soon enough that she could do things alone. Go to Toronto. Become a doctor even. There were endless possibilities once she got away. She would be so glad to be rid of them all. She'd show them that she didn't need them.

Six more months of torture and she'd be gone forever.

The door closed quietly. Marie breathed a sigh of relief. She clutched the acceptance letter and felt the exultant joy at all that it meant.

6

On a weekday in late April, instead of going straight to bed after his night-shift, Joey made a point of waiting in the upstairs kitchen for his mother's return from Mass. Coming in well after nine, she stood in the doorway for a minute and regarded him with a curious expression. It was as if she were looking at him from across a wide gulf and couldn't quite make out his features. He noticed how haggard she was, her face thin and worn, the wrinkles around her mouth more prominent. Having stopped bothering to use her dentures anymore, she looked older than ever. Her black kerchief and dress seemed to engulf her.

There was also something different about her that Joey couldn't quite put his finger on. Failing to acknowledge his concerned expression, she went downstairs to make herself breakfast.

"Ma, you were walking the tracks again, weren't you?" he said, following her down.

Pretending she hadn't heard, she busied herself making her staple of cocoa and crackers. He watched her intently from the bottom of the stairs for a minute, thinking of what he could say, trying to squeeze the simple English thoughts into his cramped Italian.

"How many more night-shifts, Joey?" she said matter-of-factly.

"Ma, I don't want you to walk the tracks. I told you."

"You don't eat all your lunch."

He gave her a sour expression.

"Why you not asleep, Joey?"

As she crushed the crackers into the bowl of cocoa Joey noticed she was wearing the same dress she had slept in. Usually she changed into another black mourning dress with matching kerchief to go to Mass in the mornings. He knew she had at least two. He had seen her washing and ironing one while she had the other on. Since the funeral he had never seen her without her mourning clothes on. If she even went outside to the garden, which was seldom, she wore her kerchief.

Without waiting for a reply she took the bowl and passed him on the stairs. She didn't smell very clean. Like a lost sheep he followed her up.

The TV room hadn't been aired yet. He could smell the foul odour of her chamber pot. She made a practice of emptying it out first thing in the morning, but it still managed to leave a lingering smell. On the end-table were days-old dirty dishes. Various copies of *Grand Hotel* were scattered about. For some reason she had taken to reading all the back issues that she kept piled on top of the Hope Chest. Her seat was sunk much lower than the rest of the sofa.

For some time now Joey had felt out of his depth. Assunta's

condition hadn't improved in the least. Contrary to Marie's assurances, it had deteriorated to an alarming degree. He couldn't understand what was happening. It was becoming virtually impossible to speak to her. And then, just recently, with the melting of the snow, she had been staying out longer than usual after Mass. One day he had seen her go right past the house, walking the tracks toward the canal.

Asked what she was doing, she said: "Seeing if the *cicoria* is out."

"But it's too early," he said.

She shrugged her shoulders.

"Ma...."

"I have to get the *cicoria, Giuseppino,*" she insisted.

It had been her practice each spring to pick dandelions in the fields just off the tracks close to the paper mill. The Canadian Pacific tracks, which went past their house, crossed over another set of train tracks about halfway to the canal. Fields of wild grass and huge boulders flanked both tracks alongside the paper mill, creating an area that abounded in dandelions. There was a bridge of not more than a 30 foot span where the elevated CPR tracks crossed over the other tracks.

As a boy he had seen his mother go out on countless occasions to pick *cicoria.* All she'd need was an apron, a bag, and a knife. Squatting down, she'd cut the leaves just above the root so it wouldn't be destroyed, fill the upturned apron, and then dump it all into the bag. They ate *cicoria* salad for days on end every spring.

Yet in the past she didn't ordinarily use the tracks to get to the fields. They were easily accessible by means of various dead-end roads. And when he had asked her why she used them she seemed not to have given it a second thought.

"*Non so,* it's faster," she said.

He wanted to say that it was dangerous, that she might sprain her ankle, but he didn't know enough Italian to express such a particular concern.

"It's not good," he said. "You're too old to walk the tracks."

Besides, it wasn't acceptable for women to walk the tracks. They were used by kids or by men going fishing in the canal. It had always been an unwritten rule in the neighbourhood that the tracks were out of bounds to any respectable woman. There was an infamous lovers' lane just at the end of the first water-bridge to the canal.

After the International bridge had been built over the fields, his mother was the only woman in the neighborhood who had persisted in picking dandelions. She could be seen at times stooping over the grass in early twilight while the huge columns of the bridge towered over her puny form. It was a practice that seemed to embarrass him more than it did her.

He was about to mention the tracks again when she finally removed her kerchief.

Joey was astounded. She had cut her own hair down to the skin, leaving large scissor marks that criss-crossed all over her head. It was such a blatantly inept job that he was left totally bewildered.

He said the first thing that came to mind. "Ma, are you crazy?" And realized just as quickly that it could possibly be taken literally now. Which stopped him short.

She looked wearily at him and said nothing for a minute. He saw how small her head was, how strange and disturbing her look—and was frightened in some deep part of him, in an area that had only been touched by his father's death.

"Ma, what're you doing?" he said, his voice shaky and unnaturally high. "How could you do a thing like that?"

"You go to bed now, Joey," she said, as if speaking to a child.

"But, Ma, what's wrong with you?"

"Go to bed now," she said calmly.

"Mamma!" he shouted.

He was so disturbed his body was trembling. The words would not come to him. She was his mother, but she could have just as well been a stranger. Almost 30 years he had lived with her, and at that moment all that time seemed to evaporate to nothing.

How could she be his mother, he thought, when he didn't even know her? He would rather have been an orphan. That way he would at least know where he stood. Instead of this. The woman who had given birth to him no more than an incubator. Adamo saying to him if he ever disparaged her ways, "She had you in her belly, Joey. She made you. She's your *mother.*" But what did it all amount to if she was actually a stranger to him? If she had lived in the same house with him for 30 years and she could still revert to barbaric customs he had no inkling of?

For a moment her eyes softened as she looked affectionately at him.

"Mamma, can't we talk?" he pleaded.

"Talk?" she said, frowning. "*Di che cosa?* About what, *giovanotto?*" She shook her hand at him in the particular Italian gesture of throwing the question back into his face.

He stared hard at her, the blood raising his voice. "Your hair."

"*Ma, stai zitto,*" she gestured to him and turned her face away in disgust. "Go to bed, Joey. Go play your hockey. Don't get into things you don't understand."

At that moment he felt such an overwhelming mixture of frustration and rage at her that he took a few steps forward and slapped her over the head.

He was so astonished at his action he could only stand there numb.

For a few seconds Assunta looked up at him like a fierce cat, her face flushing deeply, her eyes coldly defiant. He seemed to see a young woman in her. Like the photograph in Adamo's locker. Someone of another time and place who had lived another life. And whom she had kept hidden for so long. At that moment her face seemed to go into a trance, and she intoned in a dead sing-song voice the words of a song he had never heard:

Venti giorni di barca a vapore
E nel' America siamo rivati

Non abbiam trovato né paglia né fieno
Abbiam dormito sul nudo terreno
Come le bestie che va a riposà

E l'America l'è lunga l'è larga
Circondata da fiumi e montagne

After which, she seemed to lose all strength. She crumpled down into the sofa, hid her face on the armrest, and burst into low quaking sobs.

He felt the tears well up in his own eyes. He understood enough of the words to know it was an old immigrant song. Twenty days in a boat. Sleeping on the naked land. Like cattle going to rest. Surrounded by rivers and mountains. But the close proximity of his mother proved too much for him. He couldn't bear the emotion she had shown him.

Leaving without further word, he went downstairs into the cantina to escape her distressing sounds. He felt so unsettled he thought of calling Marie right then and forcing her to come back.

Joey looked around his father's bricked-in workroom in the basement where the wine and preserves were kept. Unheated year-round, it was cool and damp. The wine was kept in ginger-ale bottles in slots along the wall. There were a few empty barrels and kegs alongside the shelves of mason jars. On the other side was Adamo's large workbench that he had made himself from two-by-eights reinforced with smaller beams. Assorted carpentry tools hung on the wall above it. Larger tools like electric drills and sanders and welding torches were neatly placed underneath the bench with the paint cans and tool boxes.

Noticing the bag where he had put Adamo's mason tools, Joey emptied the contents onto the bench. The photographs had been slightly crumpled. He wiped the mortar dust off the one of his mother and brought it closer to the light.

It was hard to believe they were the same person. The young woman smiling from a farm in a village of a country he had never seen. The old woman upstairs, her hair cut to shreds, crying in front of the television.

Joey studied the face closer. There was no mistaking the strong resemblance to Marie. They were both so thin and bony, with the same sharp features and cut of hair. Marie would undoubtedly be amused if she ever saw it, he thought.

But the picture couldn't reveal more than a surface knowledge that did nothing to cool his frustration. Discouraged, he put the photograph in his wallet.

With nothing better to do, he arranged Adamo's tools neatly on the workbench.

That night they were playing their first round-robin playoff game at the Gardens to determine the Industrial League champion of the city. As soon as Joey got into his car he was able to set his mind on the game. Annalise would be watching, sitting in her usual place high in the corner. Surprisingly, coming to watch Donny play a few times had renewed her interest in sketching hockey scenes. These she'd later work over into abstracts that he found totally indecipherable. "If I'm going to live here," she said, "I might as well work with it instead of against it."

In the dressing-room Donny asked him if he had picked up the tickets to the Russian game yet.

"I forgot," Joey said.

"You better hurry up or we'll lose our subscriber's seats."

During warm-ups Joey could see that the team was ready for the playoffs. They had managed to defeat Rail Mill for the Steel Plant championship and now were playing the other winners of industrial leagues all over the city. Tonight it was a construction team. They'd play each of the three other teams twice and the one with the most points would win the overall title.

Tubby was pushing on his skates in a strutting motion, like Mussolini, his face knotted arrogantly. Beansie was doing all sorts of calisthenics like an all-pro goalie. Donny was skating smoothly and effortlessly, his face more solemn than it had ever been before a game. They had such an air of seriousness about them that they made him feel he was in the middle of the Stanley Cup playoffs. Only Boofie, who was waltzing about dreamy-eyed, detracted from the seriousness. There was a good-size crowd in attendance, creating a buzz of expectation throughout the whole arena.

Joey could feel Annalise's eyes on him as he skated around the ice. He would play as if she were the only one watching. He would play fatherless and motherless, as in the dream where there was only the expanse of ice on the lake as huge as Superior. He would forget his piddling job and his failure to make the pros and the fact he was playing on a dead-end team with the only prospect of retiring like Donny for good. But most of all, he would forget he had lost himself and had hit his own mother, because there was something happening to her that was scaring him out of his ordinary life.

In the first period both teams showed they were up for the game. Their opponents scored first on a shot from the point. Everyone came off the bench like the pros to congratulate the scorer. Then Donny scored on a quick wrist-shot from the slot and the whole Steelmaking team came off the bench too. It was tit for tat and the crowd loved it. Everyone was hollering and shouting with great enthusiasm, which stirred the players even more.

Joey felt so light on his skates that he thought he could fly. He wasn't so much caught up in the game as in his own skating. The exhilaration of stopping and starting, spurting down the wing, and then gliding smoothly over the ice made him forget everything but his dream. The feel of the wood in his hands. The clean smell of the ice. The sound of his blades cutting the surface. The smoothness under his feet that could lead him anywhere he wanted to go. Only the boards could restrain him. And when he unexpectedly found himself crashing into the wood he felt cheated that there wasn't as much room as in his dream. As much space as the whole of Lake Superior.

Tubby tried to bring him back to his senses on the bench.

"Hey...hey, Joey, what's going on? You're not playing your position. You're skating all over the fuckin' ice. What's happening?"

But he looked at him blankly, unable to answer. If there was an answer, he thought, it certainly couldn't be put into words. Anything that mattered deeply was beyond words.

In between periods Joey saw that Donny was regarding him with a knowing sad expression. Yet it was Boofie who sat down beside him in the dressing-room.

"You going on vacation?" Boofie said.

"No," Joey answered, surprised.

"Then these aren't rehearsals for vacation?"

Joey looked at him to see his expression. It was slightly whimsical and mocking. But he couldn't get angry with Boofie who hardly took anything seriously.

"What d'ya mean, Boofie?" he said.

"Your wanderings on the ice, they seem to have a quixotic air about them."

"C'mon, Boofie."

"No, I mean I can see the value of bucking the system, of parading your individuality in the face of team conformity. It takes guts, man."

"Aw, go fly a kite, Boofie."

"I'm not, but you evidently are."

And Boofie gave him that oddly twisted smile, which he couldn't really understand. Donny had told him once that there was more to Boofie than met the eye, that even though he couldn't hack it at Cornell he was more serious than he made out to be.

"Suppose," Donny had said, "suppose he was serious in whatever he said. Do you think he'd last very long on the team or in the plant?"

In a fit of reflection one time, Joey had concluded that everyone who was any good on the Steelmaking team hadn't gone all the way in hockey because of some fundamental problem in their character. With Boofie it was his inability to take anything seriously. With Tubby it seemed to be his lack of self-discipline on and off the ice. And with Beansie it was probably his lack of brains.

With himself, maybe it was more than just fear of going out on his own or loyalty to his father. Maybe it had to do with his dreams. That they were too strong—and he hadn't quite managed to live in the world outside the West End.

In the second period he picked up momentum. Even when he didn't have the puck he enjoyed pirouetting and feeling his skates crunch deeply into the ice or making the hundreds of turns that kept his eyes always on the play. So that when he finally felt the weight of the rubber disc at the end of his stick he was ready to shoot down the ice in a flash. Nothing felt better than to take a pass while coasting down the wing, put on the jets, and make a play on goal.

It was while he was skating on goal, with the defencemen between him and a clear shot at the net, that he felt the most alive. There would always be a rush of blood to his head, causing the back of his neck to tingle and his whole body to tense with excitement. So that every muscle was poised to do anything necessary to put the puck in the net. And if the defenceman was good and was looking coldly or even contemptuously at the letters on his chest instead of the puck, as he was supposed to, then he would feel the challenge even more. To somehow get around that man, or under him, or even through him if necessary. Because he was poised just as much to stop you. It was as if, Donny had told him once, he was standing between you and your paycheque. You had to use any move or trick at your disposal to get a shot at the net. So that when you were one-on-one with the goalie you were in the middle of the greatest feeling in hockey. And if you happened to be good enough and whistled the puck cleanly over his shoulder and saw the bulge where the puck hit the net and the red light flash, there was such a feeling of release that you lost yourself.

After he scored two goals in the second period no-one bothered him anymore about not playing his position. Tubby looked at him quizzically every so often on the bench, but didn't say a word. Boofie had affectionately patted him on the helmet and smiled. The other guys were just happy to be winning. Only Donny seemed to know what was happening.

Skating by him on a shift change one time, his friend had said, "You've got it all together tonight, haven't you?"

He had merely smiled back.

And when in the third period he scored his third goal, the whole bench came over and mobbed him. He could feel everyone reaching over to touch him, as if to share in some of his magic, and the suffocating joyous sensation it produced.

But in the dressing-room after the game, while everyone was congratulating him, Joey felt oddly disquieted. All his exultation seemed to vanish into thin air. He couldn't speak, and his silence detached him from his surroundings. He didn't realize what was happening until he seemed to hear the voice of his mother crying out to him. Breaking through a barrier that had somehow been invulnerable beforehand. Her voice not saying any word in particular, but her voice nonetheless. As if she were alongside him in some way. Pleading to him for something. Her hair hideously cut. Her eyes imploring him.

He was more than sorry for having hit her—but what more could she want of him to cheat him out of his moment of glory?

Later, in a coffee shop up the street from the Gardens, Annalise told him how marvellous he had looked on the ice.

"You moved so gracefully at times," she said, "you could've been a dancer."

She was leaning across the table, watching him with

intense concentration, her liquid green eyes attuned to his every shift in mood. He had always been slightly intimidated by the keenness of her perception. Her eyes virtually soaked up everything in front of her. And quickly discarded it if it didn't meet with her standards. Either a thing was "marvellous" or it was "depressing"; it either "heightened" life or "debased" it. "Marvellous not in the hackneyed way most people use the word," she said to him once. "But, 'a marvel, an astonishing and awe-inspiring thing to behold'." And she didn't spare her contempt for those things, usually pretentiously gaudy or made without feeling, which debased life. Surprisingly, the Gardens was marvellously quaint architecturally, and she rather enjoyed being with the people who came to their games. "They're what I've come from," she said.

Joey noticed how Annalise had changed. Where before she had been strong-willed and obstinate, she was now less assured, even at times nervous. Her hands trembled a little when she picked up her coffee cup. Annalise had been extremely athletic as a girl. She had a trim shapely figure that she carried with ease and a sense of suppressed energy. She still kept her straw-coloured hair short and girlish.

Only now was the bloom coming back to her cheeks. Her face was finely-featured, with milky-white skin and a dazzling smile. She looked more like an olympic swimmer than a serious artist. With her failure in Toronto she seemed to have come back to within his range, back to the girl he knew before she left home.

"I couldn't stop skating," he said. "My skates felt so light, it was unbelievable. It was like the wind pushing me."

"Let's go out and walk to the river, Joseph," she said, all of a sudden. "We can see the ice floating along the shore."

It was chilly outside. The snow wasn't completely gone from the streets. There were some dirty piles here and there, testifying to the long winter. They walked past the tracks to the mall behind the Gardens, and over to the waterfront.

"It felt so strange," he continued. "Like the times when I

was a kid at the school rink when all that mattered was playing the game and everything else was forgotten. Has your father ever mentioned the school rink where he started playing?"

"I don't remember."

"It was where we all started in the West End. Morning, noon, and night we'd skate in the cold until our bodies were like furnaces. We used to practically live on that patch of ice, learning all there was to know about the game."

She was looking up at him. "Your face and words become different when you talk about things like that, Joseph. You're usually so reticent."

He felt such a mixture of exhaustion and defeat after the events of the day that it seemed to have loosened his tongue.

"I learned my language on the ice, that's why," he said. "That's where I know things."

Annalise shook her head. "You and my father—you make quite a pair with your infernal game. Why doesn't he quit, tell me? He's an old man."

They were walking side by side. Annalise took hold of his arm and pressed against him to keep warm. She was wearing a large purple beret and a long pink scarf that reached to her knees.

"When do you feel the most alive?" Joey asked her.

"When I paint."

She said the words as conclusively as if she said she ate because she was hungry.

"Would you ever want to stop?"

"It's not the same, Joseph."

"Oh no?" he challenged her. "And how is it different?"

She tried to explain to him about the lofty aspirations of art and what it meant to her, her voice becoming warm and animated. He wasn't so much listening to the words as feeling her through his clothing. When they reached the embankment they sat on a bench where he could watch her as she talked. The soft light from a lamp overhead illuminated her face. She was so intent on her argument she lost sight of him.

When she finished he didn't know what to say. He hadn't been following closely enough. Finally, as if he had given it much thought, he said, "All you're saying is that it makes you more alive."

She thought about it for a moment. "Yes, I suppose so. But your efforts seek to enrich other people as well. I hadn't thought of it like that."

Looking at the river, they could see the large chunks of ice reflecting off the lamps along the embankment. There were hundreds of them, white and eerie, floating down the river from as far away as Lake Superior.

Joey told her about the recurring dream after his father's death. Skating on an expanse of ice as big as the largest lake in the world. The cold wind on his face. Not knowing why he was there or where he was going. The dazzling whiteness all around him.

He asked her what it could mean.

"Your face changes so dramatically."

Her voice was frank and open. He saw that her eyes were burning through him. He looked out at the river again.

"I've lived all my life in the West End," he said. "All I know of the outside world is what I see on television."

The confession was so unexpected that there was a short uneasy silence. Quickly, to erase his embarrassment, he tried to answer his own question. But his words were incoherent and stupid. He stopped before he could make a further fool of himself.

Annalise said, "Why have you never made any advances toward me, Joseph?"

Nonplussed, he smiled. "We've been closer to being a brother and sister."

The answer annoyed her. She reached over and pulled his face toward her. He felt warm breath and ice on his lips at the same time.

Joey got home in the middle of the late-night movie. His mother was fast asleep on the sofa. She looked a ghastly sight, with her badly cut hair and the abnormal tilt of her head. Her wheezing sounds of sleep were like scratchings against his skin.

"Mamma?" he called out softly.

He could still feel Annalise's kiss. Michael Rennie was walking down the street of a small American town. He had a brief-case in his hand and looked like a typical businessman. Radios were blaring the news of a Martian invasion. He appeared amused by their outrageous descriptions.

"Mamma?" he whispered.

What was he going to do with her? It was as if she had ceased to function. He had never thought she and Adamo had gotten along that well. She had never been satisfied with what he did for her. She complained constantly about everything. Every time he renovated the house she went into a litany of abuse. Any change to her surroundings was a threat to her. To move out of the neighbourhood was unthinkable. To ride in a car with her was an ordeal in itself. His father had been denied countless vacations. He had never seen his father more happy than when they would prepare their lunches in the early morning to go on a fishing trip.

On the screen Michael Rennie saw a Room For Rent sign. He entered the house and stood on the threshold as the family were huddled around the radio. The camera looked up at his ominous silhouette. The family got up startled. Patricia Neal was the mother.

"Mamma?" he called out again.

He and Marie had certainly not escaped the brunt of her discontent. But it was Marie who got the worst of it. There was nothing Marie could do that Assunta couldn't find fault with. Whether it was her high school marks that were turning her into a "snotty-nose" or her marriage to some English stranger. She had even refused to meet Richard for a long while and felt her daughter had betrayed her.

Even a year after the marriage Assunta would say, "See what happens, Joey, when you leave home. Such an *ingrata.* To a stranger even. She thinks she's so smart. Did I raise her to treat me so shamefully?"

"But, Ma, *you* left home," he said, trying to speak up for his sister.

And she'd look hurt, her face scrunching up in emotion, and say, "I had to. What do you think? You don't know, Joey."

Sometimes when she was driven to tears by Adamo after a family spat she'd say, "How can I have come here? How? I was so content in Novilara. You'll never know! Never!"

Or, earlier, when he and Marie were kids, she'd shout from some suppressed rage: "Just give me my passage money back. Let me go back to where I came from." And she'd whimper like a little frightened girl, causing him and Marie to be so afraid for her that they'd be silenced for days.

"Mamma?" he raised his voice, even now embarrassed to touch her.

When she awoke he flicked off the TV set and stood in front of her. His triumph on the ice and with Annalise had made him bold.

"Ma, this has got to stop," he said forcefully in Italian.

"What, Joey?" she said meekly, half dazed.

"You sit there all day. All day you watch television and sleep on the sofa. What's the matter with you? Are you crazy? Today you cut your hair like a crazy person. You won't sleep in your own bed. It has to stop. I don't want it anymore."

She looked hard at him for a moment, as if about to challenge him. Then, abruptly, her face went soft and pulpy.

"Joey, you hit me," she said in the whining voice of a child.

His voice didn't soften. "You made me."

"*Che cosa t'ho fatto?* What did I do to you?"

"This!" he raised his voice in anger, sweeping his hand over the room. "This is what you do to me."

"I don't bother you, Joey. This is my life."

There was a moment of silence. He could feel the anguish

of her claim start to weaken him.

"Mamma, what are you doing?" he begged.

Her face went suddenly blank and distant, as if he had questioned something she had taken entirely for granted.

"Babbo's dead, Ma," he said softly, as a simple matter of fact.

"This is my life," she said again, as if talking to herself.

"Ma," he tried to reach her, "Babbo has been dead for months. You can't go on like this."

As if she hadn't heard a word, she said, "Joey, what do you do out there?"

He was stopped short. She seemed to be talking to a sixteen-year-old she had been waiting up for.

"I play hockey, what do you think? Then I went out with Annalise."

"When you get married, Joey? Give me a grandchild?"

She was talking oddly. It scared him.

"You have a grandchild, Ma. Michael."

She made a face.

After a silence she said, "You take care of your mother, Joey?"

Her voice had a despairing, pleading quality that alarmed him.

"Don't worry, Ma," he said reassuringly, "Marie and I take care of you."

She looked away, unconvinced of his sincerity.

Her voice cold and impassive, she said, "What do you do with me now?"

"Don't speak like that," he started to raise his voice.

She looked evenly at him. "You send me back to Italia. I want to die in Italia."

"Don't talk nonsense," he said dismissively. But her voice sounded too cold.

"Yes," she said in a low resigned tone, "your father, he sent for me when I was young. Now you can send me back when I am old."

"Mamma, I told you..." he warned her.
"You hit me, Joey," her voice went soft again.
"I'm sorry, Mamma."
"You hit your own mother. What will your father say?"
"Mamma, please."

With a deadpan voice, as if speaking to herself, she said, "My own children have forsaken me. What reason is there to stay? I have never belonged here."

"Mamma, don't be crazy!"

Fiercely, her eyes blazing, she shouted, "I have never belonged here! It's true!"

It was too late to phone Marie. Besides, it had been a long day and he was exhausted. He knew now things were entirely beyond his control. He had to get his sister up sooner than expected. Perhaps she would be more effective than he was. Not only did he feel inadequate in handling the situation, but he didn't even know what she wanted of him. If it was sympathy or affection, it was she herself who had so badly trained him to convey such emotions. The situation was getting desperate. It was as if he were feeling the pull of flesh and blood from a stranger.

Up in his room, before falling asleep, he went over his day. It had been exhilarating, but very confusing. Annalise's kiss was only a dim memory. All he could look forward to was his dream.

7

"Nothing's wrong, Dad," Marie felt herself speaking down to him. "I just don't eat as much as I used to."

"But, Marie, you are too thin. You look like a sheet of paper."

He spoke in a low obsequious tone, his English worse than she could remember.

She laughed. "Don't worry. It's all right, I assure you."

"What will your mother say?"

They were in the car heading back to the Sault from the airport. Her father had been startled by her appearance when she stepped off the plane. She was wearing an old pair of skin-tight jeans and desert boots. Her long hair was coiled in an intricate mass, having been allowed to grow out on its own. She had shed her odious cocoon, looked bone-thin and gloriously herself.

Ever since leaving for university her visits home had steadily dwindled. Now she only got back for a few days during Christmas. It was just long enough to enjoy seeing Joey and her parents without opening the old wounds. And it was a welcome relief from her studies.

She looked out the window. The snow was sweeping across the bleak stretch of road. The thinner, fresher air invigorated her lungs. Her visits gave her a sense of triumph. She'd catch sight of her hometown from the plane—a patch of houses embedded in the snow. The outside world had put it in perspective. The houses appeared smaller and shabbier with each visit. She felt above it all, a visitor who could afford to be kind.

Marie wondered how long her equanimity would last once Assunta saw her.

Whenever she was back it was always interesting to see which buildings in the old neighbourhood had been demolished. It made her feel like a reigning monarch whose visit had inspired the elimination of the various eyesores along her parade route. She felt vindicated. Each visit meant a victory over her past.

Assunta was waiting for them in the basement kitchen. She had put on a good dress and was in her slippers. Her father brought down the luggage. All she had was a canvas bag. Marie instantly noticed how quickly her mother had aged, become pale and shrivelled as if something inside her had collapsed. She waited apprehensively as her mother's face went through a series of manoeuvres. Joy at seeing her. Incredulity at her appearance. Back to joy. Incredulity. Distress. Grief. And finally outrage.

Assunta raised her hands in a gesture of resignation and rushed past her, going up the stairs and leaving her words to trail behind her.

"No-one that thin could be all right," she was yelling at the top of her voice. "She looks like a ghost. Because she's living alone and doing heaven knows what. Why didn't she come home and get married like a normal girl? That's what she should do, the *ingrata*. Enough is enough. No-one should go to school that long. It's crazy! *Che bella figura!*"

And there was a slam from the bedroom door.

Adamo's face was stricken. "Why does this have to happen?" he said, looking away from her.

"It's her or me," Marie said, almost apologetically.

"Maria, Maria," he looked back to her, his eyes suffering, "what has happened to you?"

Things were quiet for the rest of the day. She changed into her muslin dress. Assunta was silent at the dinner table, observing everyone in her stiff pout. She didn't object when Marie only ate the vegetables and soup, leaving the pasta on her plate. To break the silence Joey asked her how her work was coming along. She had just finished her Masters in mathematics and was tentatively embarking on a doctorate that would take her out of math into logic and philosophy.

"It's slow in the beginning," she explained vaguely for her father's benefit as well as for Joey. Adamo had helped her financially during her undergraduate years and she felt guilty about not having repaid the debt yet. Now that she had received a substantial government grant to continue her studies she was more securely on her own two feet. "I'm in a transitional stage now, dealing more with logic than mathematics. I have to do a lot of reading before I can even think of writing. It'll take years."

"You're actually gonna be a professor?" Joey said, his tone whimsical and mocking.

Marie smiled. "That's too far into the future. Maybe."

"My big sister, a woman professor. Who would've thought."

Marie saw how Joey ate slowly, even picking at his food at times. He was still hardy and trim, but something had gone out of him. Since getting his job at the plant he had become more withdrawn and glum over the years to the point now where it seemed he didn't much care what became of him. From what she knew, he was content to live with their parents indefinitely. There had been no girlfriends since Annalise Belsito. The only times he went out were to play hockey and drink with his friends.

That night she regained her good spirits quickly. Her life seemed to have found its proper course. And she had Richard now. It was actually Richard Charlton who had been instrumental in pulling her away from pure mathematics into logic. He was already in the fourth year of his doctorate, doing work on British empirical philosophy. He had a sharp clear mind and a tenacious ambition to do original work. If things went well they'd be married when Richard received his degree in less than a year. Having separate rooms in the graduate residence on Bloor Street, they were virtually living together now, except for the large blocks of time that Richard set aside for his work.

The usual procedure for Christmas, followed since they had been kids, was to go to church first and open the gifts later. Nowadays, however, no-one but Assunta went to church anymore. Joey had long since stopped going. Assunta would slip out of the house to go to midnight Mass and come back when they were all in bed.

The evening meal had therefore become the highlight of the holidays. It was Assunta's masterpiece. In the past Marie would see her mother starting weeks in advance to prepare her special delicacies. She made tie-plates, special breads, and other assorted pastries. Marie was successful in preventing any further trouble with her mother, but she dreaded the Christmas meal.

Since her first year at university she had stopped eating Italian food altogether. Later it wasn't only Italian food, but anything having to do with her mother's particular dishes. Marie found herself unable to eat chicken anymore, or spare ribs, or steak, or broccoli, or veal, or even crusty bread. In restaurants she had to be very selective. Eventually it became so annoying that she had to avoid restaurants and cafeterias altogether. She took to reading books on nutrition and health foods, educating herself to the point where she became adept at making all sorts of light nourishing meals. Lately she had come to survive purely on such health foods as cottage cheese, wheat germ, oats, and natural yogurt.

The fact that she lost a lot of weight was an unexpected dividend. It hadn't really been uppermost in her mind. She was surprised to find herself more attractive as a result. Her skin cleared and became pinkishly lustrous. Her figure was in vogue with the taut-skinned models she occasionally saw in the New York fashion advertisements.

Only lately, however, did she come to realize that the ship she had set in motion could perhaps get out of control. Sometimes she found herself unable to eat at all. She had become somewhat highly strung, a disposition she had to control in order to think clearly. There had been occasions when she had lost her temper fairly easily and had been entirely disgusted with herself. One time she had even thrown up when Richard had forced her to eat a plate of spaghetti he had made for dinner. He couldn't understand how she could be so affected by food. It wasn't logical. But never again did he insist she eat what she didn't want.

True to expectations her mother prepared a lavish meal for Christmas dinner. There was a large basted turkey. A huge bowl of homemade ravioli. Freshly baked crusty bread. A four-layer cream cake. And many types of pastries. It almost nauseated Marie to see the rich pasta sauce on the steaming ravioli. Even the smell of the food was repugnant to her.

Everyone was dressed up. Adamo had his Sunday suit on. Joey wore his good pants and a white tie-less shirt. Her mother had permed her hair.

Adamo was talking to Joey as Assunta ladled out the pasta. As soon as Marie refused her portion there was an uneasy silence.

"Just give me a bit of the turkey, Ma," she said evenly.

Assunta pretended not to hear and put the pasta on her plate. Marie smiled.

"No, Ma, I can't eat this. Just a bit of turkey, please."

"It's Christmas, Maria," her mother said softly.

"No, Ma, I can't really," she said in English.

"Please, Maria. . . ."

Marie turned to Adamo. "Dad, please tell her I've learned to eat different types of food. More nutritious kinds. I can't eat this anymore."

Her mother unexpectedly swung her arm toward Adamo, dismissing his intervention. Her eyes grew moist as she pleaded with her again. Marie looked away, irritated. She couldn't bow to her own mother's old tactics. It was her mother or her.

She made her voice hard. "No, I said!"

Adamo gave a sign of annoyance. "Maria!"

"Please, Maria," her mother pushed her plate in front of her.

Marie had to raise her voice even more. "No, I said!"

Assunta stood at the side of the table turning stiff. Marie could feel the tension building. Right then it occurred to her that maybe she had gone too far. Her father's face told her how serious things were.

"You mean that's all you eat?" Assunta said, her voice cold and viperous. "I cook all this food, spend all this time, and you eat nothing!"

Adamo tried to calm things. "Assunta, it's Christmas. Please...."

But the tactic only served to redirect some of her anger toward him.

"*Ma,* shut up!" she screamed at him. "She comes once a year to visit us and she acts like this. Look at her. She's all bones. She can't even take care of herself. What is she doing down there? She tells us nothing. And then she comes back and acts like this! Like a snot-nose. What did we do wrong to get a daughter like this?"

Marie tried to calmly explain to her father in English.

"Dad, do you think I can come home once a year and not have to go through this nonsense? Won't she ever learn? I'm 24 and she persists in treating me like a ten-year-old. Doesn't she wonder at times why I don't come back more often?"

Adamo turned away in annoyance.

"You speak to me!" Assunta raised her voice. "Why you not speak to me? I understand!"

Joey, seeing that Assunta was beginning to get hysterical, spoke up.

"Marie, why don't you make her happy for once and just eat a little more. It won't kill you. You look like you can even use a little more."

She turned to face him, feeling her blood start to boil.

"It won't kill me, will it? Just look at you, Joey. And for the life of me I've never been able to understand why she's always tried to push the food down our throats while she eats nothing herself."

Joey made a sour face. "Maybe she's just trying to be a mother the only way she knows how."

Assunta was fuming at her.

"You can't speak to me anymore?" she said in *dialetto.* "You come into my house and you don't eat my food and you can't speak to me, your mother? You go to a big school and read many books and you act like this? An *ingrata* you are. A stranger you are. How can you be my daughter?"

Unable to bear the stridency in her mother's voice any longer, Marie shouted at her.

"*Basta!*"

"Ah, you still know Italian, then," Assunta looked scornfully at her.

"*Basta,*" she lowered her head, feeling defeated. "Enough. I can't take it anymore."

"Then eat!" she heard her mother say.

Marie looked up. Her expression had changed. "You want me to eat your food, Ma?" she said icily. "I'll eat your food. I'll show you how to eat your food."

And with that she reached her hand into the bowl of ravioli, grabbed a handful of the hot slippery pasta, and quickly stuffed it into her mouth. Assunta stared with her mouth agape. Joey made an exclamation of disgust and turned his head away. His father dislodged the table as he stood up.

Her mind was blank. She could feel the sauce flowing down her throat and onto the collar of her muslin dress. She munched on the thick gooey pasta with her cheeks puffed out wide. It took much effort to swallow. The food had an immediate effect. Her head felt it was lolling on an unsteady ship. She felt nauseated. Through a distorting mist she saw her mother's pained incredulous expression. She put more food into her mouth before her father could stop her. Her stomach began to heave. Before she could grab a napkin she spewed some of the pasta onto the table in a fit of coughing.

Giving her mother one last look she rushed upstairs to the bathroom.

After cleaning herself she felt sick and had to lie down. From her bedroom she could hear the fight in the basement. Her mother's shouts came through loud and clear. She was accusing Adamo for all the trouble. If only he had put his foot down long ago and not allowed her to leave. If only he was more forceful, and sided with her for once, instead of being so indulgent and giving their daughter money to stay away from home. If only he had not raised such ungrateful, spiteful children. None of this would have happened. The accusations became shriller and more personal. She heard Joey come up to his room and slam the door in disgust. Finally she heard Assunta give out a ghastly shriek. She wanted to be sent back to Italy immediately, she yelled. She couldn't take any more of this. They were all crazy. How could she understand them when they had grown so far apart from her? What had he gotten her into? He was to blame for having sent for her. She was happy enough in Novilara. He had ruined her life. Her own daughter hated her.

Marie felt scalding tears come down her face. The experience had left her entirely drained and defeated. It was hard to believe she could have acted so disgustingly. Her mother always seemed to bring out the worst in her. Only a couple of days back in her old world and all the years away from home had simply evaporated.

It seemed that the time spent over all those complex mathematical problems had gone for naught. Her mind had been stretched to its utmost. She had prevailed in mathematical theory, achieving such lucidity at times that she felt no problem was beyond her range. It was a comprehensible world, if one only set one's mind to unravelling its complexities. She had been captivated by the sheer power of logic. She had spent a year reading the *Principia Mathematica* of Russell and Whitehead and the collected works of Gottlieb Frege. Professors were mildly surprised and delighted that they had a woman who showed such a good grasp of theory. Marie Barone, silent "e", from the West End and of humble Italian parentage, had shown she could do the job in a field dominated by men.

As she climbed higher she had felt herself shedding her personal insecurities and self-doubts. They were like weighty baggage. And with them had gone her excess weight. She had to be light, airy, to reach the heights of the logical ladder—so that she could see the world aright.

She had escaped the West End with a vengeance. When she was having dinner with Richard in his book-lined room and discussing the explosive propositions of Wittgenstein's *Tractatus* she couldn't have been any farther away from her old neighbourhood.

Now, after a couple of days back, it seemed her old world could reduce her to a child again. Her mother hadn't changed a bit. She was like a dark immovable force that cast an overpowering shadow over her. Her presence seemed to undeniably convey that whatever Marie had gained, whatever ladders she had climbed, or however she had changed, she was still the little Italian girl who couldn't wipe herself clean.

Toward bedtime Assunta came up to confront her. Marie had kept her door shut and was reading in bed. Assunta knocked tentatively and then opened the door.

"Maria," she said plaintively, "what have I done? Tell me. Are you sick? Tell me what I done to make you like this?"

Her mother stood at the end of the bed, her face so broken by tears and perplexity that Marie herself felt a momentary impulse to break down and cry. But there seemed such a hard vein of resentment in her that she was able to control herself. She could only stare back as if mute, waiting for her mother to make the first move.

"Maria, please speak to me. What have I done to deserve this heartache? You come back only once a year and you act like this? What could I have done?"

How could she explain it, Marie told herself, if she didn't have the language? What did her mother want of her if not what she had never given her? If she couldn't say it correctly, there was nothing to do but remain silent.

For some reason her mother's vulnerability only produced an acute embarrassment. Marie couldn't look straight at her. It seemed too late for reconciliations. It had been too long a battle to make herself self-supporting.

"Maria...?"

She had been fighting her mother for so long that, even if

she wanted to, she couldn't retract now. Her course had been set.

"Maria...?" Assunta pleaded in a shriller voice.

But it was too late to be sorry, Marie almost said out loud in English. The damage had been done.

Assunta took a sudden step toward her.

"Maria, you're my daughter!" she said, in an astonished, desperate tone.

But Marie, from some part of her she had no control over, turned her face completely away from her mother and stuck it into the pillow.

Her mother emitted what sounded like an animal gasp. There was a deathly silence.

And then Assunta spoke from some deep pit in her.

"Oh, Maria, your heart has turned to stone."

The next day the house was so quiet and sullen that she found it unbearable. Even Joey couldn't look straight at her. Assunta didn't budge from her bedroom the whole day. Adamo told her Assunta was ill.

"What has happened," her father looked at her reproachfully, "it is bad, Maria, very bad. In Italia we used to have a saying: to cause bad blood between the parents and the children is to plough salt into the earth."

"Babbo, I'm sorry," she said, somewhat repentant, "but what can I do? She treats me like a little girl, has no respect for my wishes, and takes offence at the slightest thing. I have my own life to lead. She has to respect me for that or else how can I get along with her?"

"She has tried so hard to be a mother to you, Maria, you will never know. She has only wanted what's best for you."

"But she has persistently failed to see what's best for me."

Her father looked at her sadly. "Maria, you're an educated person now and you know much more than we do. But there are some things you will always be blind to. Believe me when I say this—there will never be another person in your life who will care for you as much as your mother. If you don't see that, you will never know what's the best for you."

"But, Babbo..."

"If you are so smart why have you always expected her to understand you? Why haven't you tried to understand her?"

"I've tried, believe me. But she lives in a different world. I could never speak her language."

Looking at her sternly, he said, "You don't need the language, you need to care first. Then the language is all right."

The words struck some hidden chord and made her take stock for a minute. But she couldn't sustain the feeling.

"When I build things," her father continued, "I care the way these things will help people. Then my trowel, she works good. If I don't care, my trowel works bad."

Adamo's homespun analogy caused her to smile. She arranged to fly out the next day. Assunta wouldn't come out of the bedroom to say goodbye. As if to disprove her father's accusation, Marie went to the door of the bedroom and knocked.

"Can I come in, Ma?"

There was no answer.

She opened the door and saw Assunta fully clothed and reclining on the bed. Her head was turned slightly sideways and there was an aggrieved expression on her face. She looked such a small vanquished creature that Marie felt a sudden rush of pity for her. Assunta's short black hair was dishevelled and her thin legs stuck out of her simple cotton dress like two match sticks. Had she triumphed away from home merely to get away from such a harmless creature?

"Ma, I'm sorry," she said in English. "I'm going away now. I've come to say goodbye."

Assunta turned her head and regarded her with such a sorrowfully anguished look that Marie had to avert her face. She felt terribly embarrassed. Her eyes caught the Hope Chest in the corner behind the door.

"Goodbye, Ma," she repeated, facing the Hope Chest and afraid to meet such a raw gaze.

In the short silence that followed Marie called to mind the times she had spent trying to open the chest. She had passed every test and exam that school had to offer, but she had failed to open such a simple trunk. It was ludicrous.

At that moment a series of Italian words sprang to mind. They were words she didn't realize she knew.

"*Dove la chiave del bavulo, Mamma?* Where is the key to the trunk? *Dove l'hai nascosta?* Where did you hide it? For so long I tried to find it. I looked everywhere in the bedroom. You must've found a very good place for it?"

The words came out so effortlessly that even Assunta seemed surprised. Marie saw a look of extreme puzzlement cross her features. Followed by a knowing, crafty glance directly into her eyes. But Marie had no way of knowing just what they meant. Her mother didn't answer. Above the bed the loving expression of the Sacred Heart gazed over them, his heart dripping with blood.

"*Mamma, dove l'hai nascosta?*" Marie repeated. "Where did you hide the key? It's too late now anyway."

But Assunta waved her hand, dismissing her with a look of annoyance, as if she had said the wrong thing or had said it the wrong way. Marie felt her body stiffen at the callousness of the reaction. She tried to say something in Italian, but found the words missing.

Instead in English she said sharply, "I'm going, Ma, and maybe I'll never come back."

Assunta turned her face away. Marie sensed that something irrevocable had happened.

Back in Toronto she explained to Richard why she had to return earlier than expected.

"She's absolutely incredible—an anachronism. Someone from the dark ages. And I don't know how to cope with her. She treats me like a child still. I had to do something to convince myself, at least, if not her."

"But it was such a childish thing you did," Richard said evenly.

Richard was a tall lanky man, with a boyish face that he attempted to counteract with a short goatee beard. He had fair features, not what she would call handsome but distinctive, and a shock of dark blond hair that fell over his forehead. But it was his eyes that she found the most appealing. Most often they were the calmly contemptuous and mirthful eyes of someone who was observing the chaos of the world from a lofty vantage point. At times, however, when his anger or indignation was stirred, they flashed with a proud defiance that could burn a hole through anyone. He had worked with some of the best minds in the university and had excelled enough to know exactly where he stood. Marie liked him for his scrupulous honesty and his high standards. In his presence she felt she was being led toward greater heights of awareness. He had a calm assured manner of explaining things that seemed to sharpen their blurred outlines and make them more easily comprehensible. His most contemptuous expression against a person was: "He lives in a muddle."

Marie lowered her eyes. "I couldn't help it."

"Yes, you could. It was because you lost control of yourself. And once you lose control of yourself all you are is a weathervane, subject to the dictates of any wind."

Richard's room looked over the courtyard, which was covered by a fine coat of newly fallen snow. She saw footprints from the four doors on the bottom floor converge at the main exit. A few bicycles were still quartered in the centre of the yard.

The room itself mainly consisted of books and a bed. Three of the walls had shelves from top to bottom. Richard's large desk was in the middle of the room. When he received guests he would sit behind his desk on his old swivel chair and regard them through piles of books while they sipped Courvoisier. He was so apprehensive of fire that he kept the bulk of his thesis in a small safe below the piles of old *New York Times*. The few pages that he was revising lay on his desk, along with his card files.

"What should I have done then?" she said.

She was sitting on the bed, close to the window, resting on cushions against the wall. Richard was in the guest's chair with his feet on the bed and appraising her paternally.

"You should've calmly left the table and waited for a more appropriate time to explain your position."

"You don't know my mother. No amount of explaining would work."

"It's just a matter of using the right language. Anyone can be made to listen to reason, if you use the right language and the right amount of forcefulness."

"I keep telling you that we're dealing with a person totally beyond the range of reason."

Marie had to admit, however, that it was her own fault that Richard still persisted in applying his rules to her mother. She had given only the barest of essentials on her background. She simply didn't want him to see that part of her. It had very little to do with her anymore. Apart from her periodic visits and a few phone calls, she had severed all connections with that world.

Later in the week there was a New Year's party in the basement lounge of the residence and Marie found herself drinking more than she expected. Richard found parties "vulgar affairs", but consented to come to this one to please her. She told him she had to unwind a little. The fiasco of her visit and the persistent uncertainties of switching her field of studies had left her on edge.

"Maybe I'm going into philosophy just to please you," she said.

"Don't be silly. You have a mind of your own."

But she wasn't so sure. It occurred to her that she admired Richard's mind so much that she might have hitched herself to his star.

Richard was holding court in a dimly lit corner with a

couple of older students whom she recognized as Marxists. Most of the people living in residence had gone home for the holidays. The party was for those who didn't have a home to go to or who lived too far away. They were mostly foreign students or those without families like Richard, whose parents had long ago separated and lived in different parts of the world. Or those like her, she thought, who had virtually renounced their families.

A buffet had been placed on the two pool tables, but she couldn't even look at the food much less eat it. Since vomiting in the Sault she had only been able to eat salads and yogurt. Her body didn't feel very secure on the ground. The few ryes and cokes she had drunk had produced a strange sense of euphoria. Her clothes, a simple blouse and jeans, seemed to weigh more than they should. If she discarded them she felt she'd simply rise a few inches from the ground and hover above everyone like a butterfly.

Presently a young Lebanese student whom she had seen often in the building approached her. He was dark complexioned, with long bushy hair and a lean strong body that he carried like a weapon. On more than one occasion he had kept his eye on her in such an open, frank look of desire that her knees had weakened. Because of a rape in the building the other year the courtyard entrance was kept locked at all times now, but one still had to be wary.

Looking at her unabashedly, he said, "I hope you don't mind my lack of decorum, but I've been observing you from across the room."

Marie was surprised by his good command of the language and his effrontery. His breath smelled of beer and food, and he had a day's growth of beard. Overall he looked slovenly, with old dirty jeans and unkempt hair. He was smiling at her through almost perfectly white teeth. She turned away to look for Richard, but he was engrossed in his conversation.

"I'm with somebody," she said sharply. "That man over there."

"Man?" the student said, his eyes bold and mocking.

Deciding to disregard the taunt, she moved away from him toward the magazine-room a little down the hall where a few people were sitting on the sofas. She could feel him coming up behind her. Quickly she sat beside a friend of hers and engaged her in conversation. But she found she could hardly put a few words together without sounding idiotic. Her mind felt entirely blank. The pores of her skin seemed to have opened up, letting the air flow through her body.

She had to stop talking to recollect herself.

But it was no use. A befuddling daze had overcome her mind. She put her drink away and sat absolutely still. She thought her heart would stop beating.

"We're going to get some food," she heard her friend Elizabeth say. "Do you want anything, Marie?"

She shook her head vigorously. They all left the room. She felt the Lebanese student sit beside her. He was saying something, but she couldn't make out his words. All she seemed to sense was the stale smell of food on his breath. Her body felt lighter than air.

In what seemed like only a few seconds she was gazing fixedly at the floor. Her mother's Christmas meal was laid out in all its richness not more than a few feet away. The steaming bowl of ravioli. The large basted turkey. The loaves of crusty bread. And the four-layer cream cake. She stared at it in open-mouthed wonder. An overpowering hunger seized her. The smell of the food was so excruciatingly delicious that she felt faint with dizziness. Her stomach was aching so much for it that she felt if she didn't take it right then she'd die.

Tentatively at first she reached over and touched the length of the bread loaf. It felt silky soft on the surface but firm underneath. The turkey was slippery with oil. Feeling slowly around its contours, she saw her hand inch toward the leg as if her fingers were under a magnifying glass. Abruptly she snapped it off and brought it to her mouth. The first bite sent shivers through her body. She chewed hungrily on the juicy delicious flesh that she hadn't eaten for ages. Her body arched. She could've screamed with pleasure. She couldn't have cared less if she dirtied herself. Or how obscene she might have looked doing it. Or what the outcome would be. Just gorging herself with what her body couldn't deny her any longer. All sensation focused around her mouth. Stuffing herself blind.

In no time she was gripped by an overwhelming force. She felt every muscle strain and relax with ever increasing rapidity. As if she were struggling against gravity to lift herself off the ground. Feeling her body getting lighter and lighter. Her bones melting in the warmth of the pain. Until all her body seemed to give one last heave and there was a warm delicious flood of release as she felt herself rise ever so lightly off the ground.

Richard told her afterwards that they had found her unconscious on the sofa. She was now lying on her own bed with her clothes still on. He had made her a bowl of soup and was angry at her for not taking better care of herself.

"You've hardly eaten a thing in the time you've been back," he said, his face flushed and solicitous, "and then you drink alcohol as if it were water."

Marie ate the soup slowly. She felt so weak she had trouble bringing the spoon up to her mouth. It was as if every muscle in her body had turned to sand. Richard had to sit her up in bed and feed her.

"First thing next week you're going to the clinic," he said. "You're beginning to look like an advertisement for Oxfam."

"What time is it?" she said.

"Eleven-thirty."

"Bring me some cottage cheese from the fridge."

She ate slowly as much as would go down, feeling her light-headedness dissipate and some vigour returning to her limbs.

At twelve she kissed Richard and they toasted in the new year with a glass of milk.

"This is going to be the deciding year," he said.

"I believe you."

He mentioned a few routine worries about his thesis. Then his face changed abruptly. He looked at her with his fierce inquisitive expression.

"What happened in there, Marie?"

"I must've fainted."

"What was that Zukoor fellow doing in there?"

"I was talking to Elizabeth, and then she left and I must've been talking to him when I lost consciousness."

"Elizabeth said she came back and found the door closed."

"Really? I don't remember."

"If he did anything..."

"Nothing happened, Richard. I just fainted from weakness. It's not the first time."

"You're going to the clinic the first day it opens. This not eating has got entirely out of hand."

Marie consented to see a doctor. She wasn't sure of what had happened. And that frightened her more than any of the possibilities. The only way to be sure was to talk to the Lebanese student. But she didn't think she could ever face him again. Besides, how could she believe what he said? She had lost control of herself. That was the unpardonable sin. It all seemed like an unbelievable hallucination.

Later that night when Richard was bending down to kiss her goodnight she pulled him onto the bed and asked him to stay.

"I'm still afraid," she said.

They made love. Richard expressed concern about her condition, but she seemed to be all right. She didn't feel particularly excited, just needed some comfort and cuddling. Richard was ardent enough, and seemed to try very hard, but he could never bring her to the point where she lost herself. Perhaps it was because she still couldn't give herself over to him. She realized it would take a total surrender, which she had never done, and perhaps was incapable of doing. She didn't know.

They were still rather shy and tentative in their love-making. Richard seemed to give each part of her body an equal share of his attention, as if he were apportioning his duties accordingly. Not surprisingly, it made her overly self-conscious, so that she'd be marking the time before he moved to the next part of her. He didn't seem to notice even that she wasn't entirely with him but still in her mind, curiously detached.

Every so often she moaned and led him to believe she was with him—she couldn't deny him that. It was one of the things that came instinctively. And it wasn't entirely to please him. For it helped him to increase his ardour, which in turn made her enjoy the best part of love-making. That time when she made him finally lose control of his movements so that he became a frenzied little boy entirely in her power.

She liked to stroke his hair afterwards and feel him spent and breathing hard on top of her. It was the time she felt closest to loving him—when he seemed entirely shorn of his defences and was naked to her.

Later, when Richard was asleep, Marie lay awake facing the ceiling, her hot tears splashing silently onto the pillow. She felt as disheartened as she had ever felt in her life. There was something wrong with her. She could feel it in her bones—something so deep and so much a part of her she couldn't bring it to the surface. Or else how could she lose control of herself like that at the party? It shook her more than she cared to admit. Richard was right. She was wasting away to an alarming extent. When she tried to eat more than she was used to she'd vomit up the food. Some days she didn't eat a thing. Her flesh seemed to be melting away from her, as if her bones were too hot for her body. And now this frightening hallucination that had seemed so vivid. She hadn't been so excited in her life. It was the second time she had come without touching herself.

Marie felt for Richard's hand and brought it to her face.

Her father's words came back to her: there will never be another person in your life who will care for you as much as your mother.

It couldn't be true, she thought, rubbing her tears away with the back of Richard's hand. Assunta had never shown the slightest bit of affection toward her. She had only known how to frustrate and bully her. Into becoming a perfect Italian wife and mother. Complete with the fat and martyred disposition.

At that moment Marie felt the unmistakable presence of her mother's dark thin figure in the room. She felt it amongst the books and plants. Amongst the desk and chairs, and in her papers with all the complex mathematical solutions. She felt her in the walls that were covered with posters and prints she had accumulated to display her culture and refinement. And in the strange man sleeping beside her who would take her even further away from all she had been brought up on.

Her mother: ignorant and implacable in her ways. Her face sorrowfully aggrieved. A person whom she had always been at odds with.

Adamo's words one time when she had angered him to the point of tears: no matter what you are, what you become, Maria, she had you in her belly. How can you fight the blood in you, *ignoranta*!

There was a hollow sinking feeling in her stomach, as if it were full of poisonous juices. She sat up in bed, feeling nauseated, her body starting to quake. In a minute she was in the bathroom retching up all she had eaten that night.

"Mamma," she said out loud, the tears streaming down her cheeks, "Mamma, I don't even know you."

Even more food than she had eaten seemed to come up. She could smell the ravioli and the turkey of the Christmas dinner in the sickening greenish bile that had poisoned her from the very beginning. Sitting on the floor over the bowl, she felt her whole insides wanting to come out. Her stomach heaved again and again, but nothing would come out anymore.

Marie got up and looked at herself in the mirror. Her face was old and ravaged. It was as if her mother were staring back at her.

"Mamma," she said. "Mamma, I'm sorry."

8

One day in early April the widow Angeline dropped in and told Joey she had finally come to terms with the city and had sold her house. She'd move into the senior citizens' home down the street at the end of the following month.

"You're the last holdout now, Joey," she said. "You better give them what they want or they will take it away from you at a lower price."

He was surprised by her sudden turnabout. He figured both houses could hold out together and delay the urban renewal people so long that they'd perhaps have to change their plans. Just recently he had had numerous visits from the planners. They had quoted figures, which were more than reasonable, and schedule plans, which they said could hardly be delayed by the two houses. Another apartment block was scheduled to go up in the fall. Now it would be virtually impossible to hold out alone.

"But I thought you were going to stay another year," Joey said.

The widow shook her head sadly. "My kids think I should move out now, Joey. They don't want me to be all alone in the house. They think I'm too old. If anything should happen there would be nobody there."

Awkwardly he said, "Did they ask you to go to the home?"

"No, I want to go myself. The young people, they're still young. They want me to move in with them, but I say no.

They have their own life. As long as they come to see me, I don't mind living alone. When Eugenio left I learned."

"I don't know what to do now," he said.

"You've got to sell, Joey."

He looked at her and then directed his eyes toward the ceiling of the basement, below the TV room.

"I don't think she can move out right now," he whispered.

Joey remained in the basement while the widow Angeline went up to speak to Assunta. He could only hear the drone of their conversation, with long meaningful silences in between.

He went into the cantina and got a bottle of wine. His father's mason's tools were still on the workbench where he had left them weeks ago. They lay there unchanged, proclaiming visibly an undeniable fact. Joey wondered what his father would do about the house—and about Assunta. Only the man who had built the house, he thought, should make the decision to have it torn down. Lying still and long unused, the tools emphasized the absence of his father. And the spot Adamo had put him in.

He looked closer at the tools, as if there was more they could say to him. They seemed not to have had their last say yet.

Joey was on his second glass by the time the widow came down to speak to him again. He heard her taking the stairs very carefully. Her legs were in a bad way. But she still had a lot of life in her. Unlike most of the neighbourhood women her age, she had stopped wearing her mourning clothes not long after Eugenio's death.

"You can't serve omelettes dressed like a hearse," she said.

Only on Sundays would she put on the full regalia of a Black Madonna, out of respect for her husband.

The widow had been living in the neighbouring house long before his father had moved in. She had raised all her children in the West End. Even though the younger ones were a little older than he was, he could remember playing with them for a number of years before they went to high school. Every Sunday either a son or a daughter would come with a car full of grandchildren to pay her a visit. Her grandchildren called her Nonna Angie, and she'd delight them with games and stories. Joey had seen her in the backyard on all fours with two tots on her back playing horsie. Yet she could be firm and authoritative. She'd fly into a rage if she thought her grandchildren were being raised improperly. Once he had seen her openly reprimand a daughter of 35 for not spanking a disobedient ten-year-old. And had promptly spanked the child herself.

He regarded her silently as she reached the table. For so many years Assunta had envied Angeline her adoring grandchildren. It was so unfair, he thought.

"Give me the bottle," she said, shaking her head sadly. "In two years I'll need a wheelchair."

She poured the wine straight and drank like a young man.

They were silent for a moment, each collecting his thoughts.

"I don't know about you, Joey," she said in her deep, gravelly voice. "You're close to 30. Still playing hockey. Still not married. What's wrong with you? *Testa dura* is what you have, hey? Just like my youngest, Rena. She comes home from Montreal every Christmas. She's 31. Why you not married yet? I tell her. Men are afraid of me, Momma, she laughs. She's a big-time doctor. She handles the wealthy people. But she's not married. What's going to happen to the family if the young people don't marry and have kids? What's going to happen to the old people who have no grandchildren? Tell me."

He looked at her blankly.

"Young people..." she shook her head wearily. "They're so smart, but they don't understand much. Why don't you move out of the West End? Rena tells me every year. I raised all of you here, I'll die here, I tell her."

"What did my mother say about your moving out?" he

anxiously asked her.

The widow looked up. Her face became downcast.

"She's so changed, Joey. It's hard to believe the way she cut her hair. I remember seeing things like this in the old country. But not here. And I've been here a long time now."

"Did she say anything?" he repeated.

"She just looked at me in a strange way and said the time has come."

"Time for what?"

"I don't know. She hardly speaks to me now. I do all the talking. I see her walking the tracks and I say to her, 'Sunta, why do you walk the tracks?' She just stares at me. She's getting in a bad way, Joey. You have to look out for her. Just now she started to cry. Asked me if I wanted to go back to Italy with her?"

Joey looked alarmed.

"Oh no, I can't go back. It's been too long for me. Here is where my children and grandchildren are."

He gulped down his glass.

The widow placed her hand on his arm. "Talk to her, Joey. Make her understand her life belongs here."

"I just can't send her back," he said abstractly.

After six, before going to the Russian game with Donny and Annalise, Joey phoned Marie and told her about the widow's decision and the possibility of moving out himself.

"What'll we do about Mom then?" he asked her abruptly.

"How much are they offering for the house?"

He quoted the figure that, even though reasonable, could never reflect his father's care and pride for the structure. It had been an oversized shack when they first moved in. No basement. Grossly unpainted and neglected exterior siding. Sagging floors. Curled linoleum. Rotting wood all over. A garbage dump for the backyard. Only through painstaking work, room by room, year by year, did his father get it in the shape it was now in.

"Can you buy a new house with that?" she said.

"I don't know. I never thought about it. What would we want with a new house anyway?"

"What about an apartment?"

"Listen, Marie, I don't know what to do. You gotta help me. You don't seem to realize how much she's changed. She's just given up. She doesn't do anything anymore. All she does is sleep, watch TV, and go to church. Now she goes out by the tracks and walks in the fields. Says she's picking *cicoria,* but she hardly comes back with any."

There was a short pause.

"What about the old-age home?" Marie said.

"What about it?"

"Don't be dense, Joey."

In the short silence that followed he strained to hear whether Assunta was listening.

Joey lowered his voice. "You gotta be here, Marie. I can't do this alone."

"It's not as if it would be such a drastic move would it?" Marie said. Her voice was matter-of-fact. "The place is just down the street."

Joey said indignantly, "I'm not doing anything till you come back in June."

"Just be patient a little while longer, Joey. We'll take care of it when I get back there. I'm becoming entirely disillusioned about this city anyway."

"Maybe you can let Mom take care of Michael," he said, the idea suddenly striking a ray of hope.

"I don't know," she hesitated.

"Sure." He was excited by the idea. "That could do the trick. She's always needed someone to take care of, you know that. You could work and let Mom take care of Michael during the day."

"I don't know. He's afraid of her."

"What're you saying, Marie, for Christ's sake? He doesn't even know her. You've brought him up so few times. Give her a chance. She loves Michael. You don't know."

"She has her old ways..."

"Why don't you tell her on the phone right now, hey? It'll cheer her up so much. C'mon..."

There was a pause. The more he thought about it the more excited he was about the idea. It could be the very thing to snap his mother out of her apathy. And he wouldn't mind taking care of his nephew either. Maybe teach him some hockey. All the moves. Make him a pro star.

When Marie spoke her tone was tentative. "Listen, Joey, I can't speak to her on the phone. But you tell her there's a possibility of my getting a job in the Sault and that maybe she can take care of Michael...babysit...do things like that, all right."

When he told Assunta, the news didn't seem to sink in the way he thought it would. She looked at him blankly, as if she didn't believe him.

"Michael...he's coming to this house, Ma," he said in dialect. "You have to...care for Michael...at the time Maria is working. She said so. At the end of June. That's good, no? You get to recognize him. I teach him how to play hockey. It's good, no?"

She didn't say anything, her face hard and unyielding. Even though some of her hair had grown back, it still gave her a wild crazy look. He hadn't been able to persuade her to go to the hairdressers.

"Ma, c'mon, this is what you always wanted," he said in English. "To take care of little Michael. Maria's bringing him back, believe me. Maybe things will be all right between you and Maria. You can't go on like that with her. You gotta stop all this."

He swept his hand over her and the room and the TV set.

Not seeming to have heard a word he said, she looked at him fiercely. "Send me back to Novilara."

"Ah, Ma."

That night at the hockey game his mind was so preoccupied with the idea of Michael and Marie coming back that he didn't pay close attention to the first period. Donny was studying the Soviets thoughtfully. Annalise had her sketch pad and was sketching intently. Not only the players these days, but the people in the crowd as well. She had taken to wearing the common clothes of the city: nylon ski jacket and denim jeans. Gone were her few attempts at flamboyance like the scarves and berets.

Joey was convinced now that if he could hold out a few more months with his mother, things would turn for the better once Marie came back.

"They're skating rings around us," Donny said in between periods.

The Soviets were leading 4-0. It was no contest.

Annalise said, "They're as marvellously conditioned as the Bolshoi."

Donny gave him a wry look.

In the second period Joey temporarily forgot about his mother and concentrated on the way the Soviets played. It was a joy to watch their skating and passing—rhythmical and clean, without a waste of energy. And when they got into the offensive zone, they whipped the puck around so quickly and unexpectedly that they had the Juniors befuddled. Joey could clearly see that they played as a very efficient unit, so that if any individual stood out it was because of the play of the unit. Knowing where their teammates were at all times, they could pass the puck without even looking. They wouldn't shoot the puck on goal unless there was the best chance of scoring. The man who scored was merely the last one to touch the puck. He even seemed a little embarrassed to be singled out with that distinction.

When he pointed that out to Donny, his friend only shrugged.

"Sure," Donny said, "scoring isn't important—winning is. We all want to win. What I want to see is whether they've made the game better or worse in order to win."

Joey really didn't know what his friend was getting at.

Hockey was hockey. You played with skates and stick. The object of the game was to put the puck into the net more times than your opponent. The Soviets were damned good. They were putting the puck into the net many more times than the Juniors. And the way they did it was good to watch.

Somehow the idea brought his dream to mind. What was he doing with the puck in the middle of Lake Superior, if indeed it was Lake Superior? There was no-one to pass to, there was no-one to help him. There was only the dazzling, smooth ice all around him, untouched by any other skates. Maybe it would blind him. Maybe it would crack and let Superior swallow him up.

The only times he could remember being anywhere close to Lake Superior was on fishing excursions with his father north of the city in the bays and inlets that formed the funnel of the huge lake as it passed into St. Mary's River. They'd be in their boat for hours, with the lines sticking obliquely in the shimmering water, and not mention much more than the state of the weather.

About halfway through the third period Donny abruptly announced he had seen enough and wanted to leave.

"What's the matter, Dad?" Annalise said. "There's still a lot of time left."

"The game's over," he said stiffly, as if he had made up his mind about something.

Joey tried to persuade him to stay, but Donny was oddly inflexible. After the Steelmaking team had won the city championship Donny hadn't been himself. Instead of whooping it up with the rest of the fellows he had gone off to the corner to be alone. In the weeks that followed Joey had seen him morose and distant at work.

They walked down to ice level and followed the sweep of the boards toward the side exit. The packed arena was following the play on the ice, captivated by the extraordinary dexterity of the Soviets.

Before Joey could realize it, however, Donny had passed

the exit and was heading resolutely for the Soviet bench.

Joey quickly looked at Annalise. "Where's he going?"

She shook her head. He saw a look of alarm pass over her features. Without thought he went after his friend in case he did anything foolish.

A few civilians with authoritative expressions were milling about the bench area. Before Joey got there Donny had somehow explained something to them and gotten through. He went directly behind the bench and stuck his program and a pen up to a man in a stylish turtleneck sweater and leather jacket sitting in the stands. Joey recognized him to be the international star of the team who was sitting out the game. The Soviet player seemed a little surprised but signed his autograph nevertheless. While he was doing this some players on the bench turned around to see what was happening. Donny seemed to study their faces for a minute, as if he were preparing to speak. They looked at him suspiciously. But his face broke out into a friendly smile and they smiled back.

Outside in the parking-lot Donny said, "I just wanted to get a closer look."

Annalise laughed. "We thought you were going to seek some sort of revenge on them for beating us so badly."

Donny didn't think it was a laughing matter. He looked evenly at them, his face earnest.

"I'll tell you what I saw," he said to Joey. "When I went right up to them and looked into their eyes. And I knew it all along too. Damned if I didn't know it."

And he nodded his head, smiling cryptically as if he had been privy to a great secret.

Joey could smell the fresh aroma of newly grown grass. It was the end of another season. Now there was only the long interminable wait for the next one. Life would slow down, lose its spark, become dull and routine again.

"Well?" Joey said, knowing that Donny wanted to be set up for his opportunity.

"They didn't have the McFadden rink in their faces," he

smiled.

Before they could ask him what it meant he waved and was off. "See you at the Vic. I have something to tell you."

In the car Annalise asked him about the McFadden rink.

"It's where your father and I started playing," Joey said, feeling his old familiar emotions well up. "Only an outdoor neighbourhood rink with a shack and a pot-bellied stove. But much more than that to us."

In the silence he tried to collect his thoughts, but it seemed the words were so tied up to his feelings that they came out entirely without effort—as if he had given himself over to his most natural juices.

"I don't know if you've ever seen this type of shack. They don't build them anymore, as far as I know. Now they build small indoor arenas where the kids start playing organized hockey complete with coaches and strategy at five years old. But back then the neighbourhood rink had a simple wooden shack, partitioned into a girls' and boys' side with swing doors and no windows. Each side had a pot-bellied stove in the middle of the room and benches all around—although I have to admit I never got a peek at the girls' side until I was much older. When the girls went through those swing doors they were as out of bounds as if they had stepped into a prayer book."

"The shack would be like a snug womb when we came in from the cold. My skin would be burning and my nose would be white and dripping and I'd sprawl on the bench and dig my skates into the floor—waiting for the heat to thaw me out. The stove was kept so hot at times it would glow red in its belly. Sometimes the guys would take the snow off their blades and toss it on top of the stove where it would sizzle and steam. If you went too close to the heat you'd thaw too quickly and really feel the pain—like your skin was on fire. Then the guys would talk or horse around, or if they had played particularly hard just breathe quietly before going out into the cold again. Carved all around us were the initials and declarations of love that made us feel we were part of a tradition. Because they brought the same shack back every winter. It was our shack, and there was nothing sadder to see with the approach of spring than that shack raised on a platform and being hauled out of the neighbourhood."

"Where was it taken to?" Annalise said, her voice low and sympathetic.

"We never knew. It was taken away and each winter we saw it back again. But the rink was more than that shack. It was the hub of social activity in the neighbourhood during the long winters. It was where you met friends, started noticing girls, and heard the latest news. It was where you first started to prove yourself by learning how to swear and smoke and fight over girls. Which I don't do to this day. In the evenings, during skating hours, any guy worth his salt in the West End would slick down his hair, put some Juicy Fruit in his mouth, sling his skates over his shoulders and tramp off to the rink to show his stuff. He'd skate around the rink at the beginning in loping strides just to show what he could do, indifferent to the stares of the girls who usually skated in groups, and then swoop past them just to let them know he wasn't missing anything. Later, when he got tired of showing off, he'd eye the particular girl he had a fancy for and brush by her every time he made a turn. If she didn't snub him he knew he had a conquest. Then they'd skate hand-in-hand and be the envy of everyone.

"But most important, the rink was where you held your first stick and skated awkwardly after a small rubber puck for some reason that took your breath away. Then you played day after day, into the cold winter evenings, till you had developed the fundamental skills that stayed with you for life. We played shinny pick-up games where we'd stay on the ice for hours at a stretch and go only as hard as our natural juices carried us. There was no need to show somebody that you wanted to win beyond anything. It was as if the rink was out of bounds to the adult world. There were so many guys on the ice at one time that you'd learn to stickhandle through twice as many players as on an ordinary team, weave and pivot with twice the ordinary speed, so that when you finally played organized hockey you'd be surprised at how much ice space you had to manoeuvre on. And before every game, and many times alone when no-one else was on the ice, you'd rifle the puck against the boards or the net, practising all the different kinds of shots you needed to improve your game."

He stopped, feeling embarrassed at having talked too long. Annalise was looking intently at him. After easing the car into the parking-lot, he shut off the motor and remained still, staring ahead of him.

Annalise gently touched his arm. "Don't stop. There are things in you, Joey, that you've kept inside too long."

"I never shoot my mouth off like this." He put his face down on the steering-wheel. "But I can't help it."

"Don't stop," she whispered.

"It's as if I'm starting to remember the things I long forgot."

"Like you're reawakening from a sleep," she said.

"Yes. Ever since my father's death."

"When things aren't in front of you anymore you see them in a different way, that's all. I used to hate the vulgarity of this city, for example. The steel plant. The sports. The high school mentality. Until I was away for a while and I learned the city had made me what I was and I was only fighting myself."

"But at least you got away for a while. I had a chance to do something with my life—play professional hockey—and I blew it."

"Oh, come off it, Joey," her voice rose irritably. "Do you know how many guys there are in this city who still think they could've made it? Or in this country? How many failed hockey players? Just ask my father."

"It was your father who sparked all our ambitions at the rink," he said indignantly. "It was Donny Belsito who made it to the pros. If one guy from the West End could make it, then anyone could. He charted the map for us. We used to hear stories all the time about him. He brought success so close to us we could taste it."

"Why did he come back and work at the plant then?"

Joey was alarmed at the question.

"He was injured and couldn't play anymore."

Annalise's face softened. She was looking anxiously at him.

"It was because he couldn't stand the business-like nature of the sport anymore. Yes, he was injured, but that wasn't it." She shook her head as if she knew only too well. "He liked the game too much. He's like you, Joey, a sentimentalist at heart. You've heard him speak about the game, you should know. The purity and the passion of it all—that sort of thing. He simply couldn't stand what the game was like in the big leagues—business and politics and winning at all costs. And that's one of the reasons I like my father so much."

She was looking at him in such a tender open way he felt himself drawn into her arms. Something seemed to dissolve inside him, some undigestible bile that had long been poisoning his body. He felt Annalise kissing him hungrily, felt her firm breasts pushing into him, and was momentarily released from his thoughts.

Of the few women Joey had known he was always surprised by the amount of passion he could engender in them by the slightest effort on his part.

They found Donny sitting alone in the lounge waiting for them.

"Where have you been? I've already put one down."

He seemed to have recovered his good spirits. After their drinks came Donny raised his glass.

"Here's to my retirement from hockey."

They looked warily at him, unable to tell whether he was serious.

"What do you mean, Dad?" Annalise said.

Assuming a mock pose, he said, "I've called this press

conference to officially announce my retirement from the game."

He was smiling, but the edge in his voice told them he wasn't joking. He continued in his mocking, self-deprecatory tone, mimicking the speeches of the great athletes of the past about how much the game meant to him and who was responsible for his rise to fame, until abruptly his voice changed in mid-sentence and he wasn't fooling any longer.

"I'm 46 years old," Donny said, his voice breaking slightly.

The unexpected show of emotion made them silent. Annalise was looking fixedly at her father, her eyes bright and loving.

"When you play a game for a long time," Donny continued, recovering himself, "you tend to remain a kid for a long time. Your body starts to go on you, but in your mind you stay that kid who played the game when he was twelve years old. You grow up, raise a family, and assume the responsibilities of parenthood, but still in some deep part of you there's that twelve-year-old kid hollering and screaming in the cold wind of the outdoor rink. And you never want that kid to grow up or change because, somehow, he's the best part of you. Everything else about you has fallen into the routine of everyday concerns. You've become like everyone else, you earn money and make children and become important, everything that you thought fantastic when you were young, but somehow... not the same afterwards. But that kid...that kid had something that can't be shared with anyone else, something that was his alone and makes him different from everyone else. What it is I don't know. But I do know I was never as alive as I was then."

Donny looked at Joey searchingly. "Don't you know?"

Joey shook his head, unable to speak. It couldn't be put into words anyway, he thought, so there was no use in trying. Yet he knew what Donny was talking about. He knew just as surely as he knew his dream.

Looking away from Donny, he noticed that Annalise's face was flushed with excitement. She was looking raptly at her father. It was as if her face were radiating an inner force that was bursting to get out. Somehow the way she was looking at her father touched him like nothing else before. Not aware of his presence there, she showed him something he had never seen in her. She seemed so full of energy, so alive, that he was suffused with an uncontrollable longing for her. Later he was to think that that moment of seeing her as she looked lovingly at her father told him everything he needed to know about her.

Being in an expansive mood that night, Donny told them stories of his year in the pros and some of the funnier incidents from the Steel Plant League. At one point he became emotional again when he recounted the day Annalise was born. It occurred during his year in the minor leagues while he was on a road trip.

"I had asked the doctor to have someone phone me immediately when it happened. And here we are in Rochester losing 2-0 in the third period when our trainer comes up to me at the bench and tells me Nicole has just had a baby girl. Well, I starts whooping right on the bench like crazy and the whole arena stares at me as if I'm off my rocker. So the coach—an old crew-cut who played with Howie Morenz—comes up to me and fines me $100. 'I just had a baby girl,' I says. 'I don't give a shit if you had a baby gorilla,' he says. 'That'll cost you $100. We're losing, dammit.' So I went out on the ice and proceeded to score three goals to win the game, my skates five feet off the ground all the while. And then I went up to the coach and said, 'We're not losing anymore, coach. How about killing that fine as a gift to the new papa?' And he stares at me as if I had stolen his cigar and says, 'Kid, I never went back on a fine in my life.' 'Coach,' I says, 'I've never been a father in my life.' "

He stared at Annalise for a while, his eyes getting misty, and Annalise put her arm around him, and shook her head with a big smile on her face.

Later they had to help Donny to his car, although Joey didn't feel too steady on his feet either.

"I'll drive him home," Annalise said after she closed the door.

"Wait a minute. I have to ask him something."

Joey opened the door and looked down at his long-time idol.

"Donny," he said, "I want to ask you a question. The answer means a lot to me, so please tell me the truth. Did you leave the pros on your own or was it because of your injuries?"

Donny looked up at him wearily. "I'm drunk, Joey, but I'll tell you one thing. You still have that kid in you. The pros would only have killed him."

He kissed Annalise goodnight, feeling the cool breeze fanning his hair.

"There's so much to paint now," she said.

When he got home at 2 he found the TV room vacant. The light and set were on as usual. Everything looked normal, except that his mother was absent. He immediately went to the bedroom, expecting her to have finally come to her senses, but he found that empty as well.

"Ma, where are you?" he shouted. "I'm back."

He checked the house from top to bottom. Then he went outside and checked the windows of the widow Angeline's house. Everything was pitch dark. He didn't feel very clear-headed.

Going back into the house, he phoned a few people in the neighbourhood whom she might have visited, but they had no idea where she was.

For the first time since his father's death he had a terrible urgency of how deserted the house was. And how fragile, now that its existence was in the balance. Something that had been solid and secure as the care that framed it now seemed on the verge of tottering.

Feeling that the situation required him to be sober, he

boiled some water for coffee.

Joey decided to drink his coffee and wait in the TV room. It was possible that she had merely stepped out somewhere and would be back shortly. But after half an hour he started to get worried. The more he sobered up, the guiltier he felt. He shouldn't have been out so long, for one, he thought. It occurred to him that he might have been neglecting her, that he hadn't done enough to understand her situation. Maybe he should have put her in a nursing home or an old-age home where other people were more qualified to take care of her. It was all right when Adamo was alive. Like a buffer, his father was able to cushion them from their mother's old-fashioned ways, her intractableness, her hard bitterness at having come to the new country, and her sense of doom about everything. She was highly strung, demonstrative and stubborn. He was calm, reticent and flexible. Now that Adamo was gone Joey could feel just how wide the gulf between them actually was.

Unable to wait any longer and feeling somewhat sober, he decided to look for her. He left a note in phonetic spelling in Italian in case she came back while he was out. First he checked around the house and in the garage. Then he walked up the street toward James. All the lights were out in the old-age home except for the lamp over the front door. The streets were entirely deserted—all the cars parked neatly in the apartment lots. The wind had picked up and the air was chilly.

In his peculiar state Joey was struck by the images of the apartment buildings against the glow of the full moon. They were like gravestones marking gigantic graves. And the parking-lots beneath them were the flowered mounds of earth that covered the West End.

Not much later he felt a cold damp hand sink through his back and curl around his spine. He twisted around, but there was no-one there. A sudden chilling dread overcame him. It was of nothing in particular, but it was so intense he was shaking. He had a sickening premonition that everything he knew was really tenuous and unimportant. His mother. Annalise. Hockey. The house. The West End. Donny Belsito. They all seemed to slip away from him. Since they existed they could just as easily cease to exist. Everything, including his own life, could be pulled from under him at any second.

He began to run as fast as he could down the street. He ran quickly past Queen, down to the end of one of the plant parking-lots, to where James curved toward the tracks and into a dead-end. There were no streetlights this far down. Hardly able to see where he was going, he stopped to catch his breath.

He could feel the sweat coming down his back. Breathing easier he took short tentative steps up the path that led to the tracks. At the bottom he could see the sweep of the International bridge that rose just above the tracks. It was supported by huge concrete pillars that broadened out at the top. Farther to his right, where the bridge steeped higher over the canal, the supports changed into gigantic arches. Not more than ten yards to his right the ground dipped steeply into the ravine of the other tracks that crossed under the small-trussed train bridge. As he climbed higher to the elevated tracks the paper mill came into view, with its stockpile of logs and the silhouette of its smokestack.

He felt the stiffer, chilly wind when he got to the top. From the higher vantage point he had a good view of the fields on either side. The sparse lighting on the International bridge, as well as the faraway lights of the canal and the glow of the moon, gave him some help, but he couldn't see very far into the fields. Joey looked down onto the other tracks in both directions. There wasn't a soul in sight. He hadn't used the pathway over the tracks since he was a kid. Looking for Indians and adventure. Then going to the canal to see the lakeway freighters carrying cargo from Thunder Bay and Duluth. Ships that appeared gigantic when they were within reaching distance in the narrow slits of the locks, but would be specks of smoke and steel in the reaches of Superior. He had seen them from the high promontory at Gros Cap west of the Sault inching their way out of the channel and into the vast lake.

His memories. The fields where he roamed as a kid. The vast area on the shores of Superior and St. Mary's river. The sure solid ground of his home. He seemed to be regarding it all in a different light now, as if he were seeing something that had escaped him all the time he had been living there. As if, as Annalise said, he was awakening from a sleep.

But if to awaken meant he would be vulnerable to the dread he had just felt then he'd just as soon sleep indefinitely.

He was just about to turn back when he spotted a figure approaching on the length of the tracks from the canal. It appeared to have emerged from the darkness. Joey stood transfixed by the strange and ominous sight.

The figure was approaching very slowly, at such a deathly pace that he wondered if he wasn't in fact seeing an apparition. There was a mechanical evenness to its steps. He realized the figure was taking the track ties one at a time.

He felt himself shivering, unable to move. In his mind, though, he was skating faster than ever on the ice of Superior, feeling the cold wind burn his face, the horizon unbroken in all directions.

Joey waited with a sense of doom. He could tell as it got nearer that it was a woman, and that, when closer, an old woman camouflaged in black.

It was no use going back to sleep, he thought. He could never escape the Black Madonna, no matter how much he skated.

His mother came right up to him, as if she had been expecting him all along. He was speechless at her appearance in the darkness. She held out her hand to him as if she would offer him anything he wanted.

9

When the final bell went Marie lay back in her seat and watched her students stampede out the door. It had been such an exhausting day that she decided to cancel her special math class after school. Writing a note to that effect, she taped it to the outside of her door and waited for Carlo Spina.

Carlo was a grade-eleven boy who had been giving her trouble all term. Somehow he had taken a violent dislike to her and never missed an opportunity to get on her nerves, often to the point of openly defying her. Her inquiries had revealed that his other teachers weren't having particular trouble with him. She had sent him to the principal twice already and one more time would mean a temporary expulsion. Although he wasn't a bright student, he did take part in school affairs and seemed conscientious and well-mannered outside her classroom. Today he had openly refused to answer a question in such an insolently hostile manner that she had been provoked into striking him across the face. After which he had stormed out of the classroom. The whole thing had got out of hand, and she had to settle matters before he made her a nervous wreck.

As soon as he came in he seated himself without any prompting in the desk in front of hers and assumed a cocky disrespectful pose. He was a short wiry boy, dark and unmistakably Italian, with well-groomed curly hair and some fuzz under his nose where he was attempting to grow a moustache. Unlike most of the other boys, he was usually well dressed in school, wearing tapered white shirts and tight imported pants. The other boys called him Spiffy, and he seemed to revel in being acknowledged different in a school where most of the other Italian boys were more or less indistinguishable from the rest. The school, on the corner of Bloor and Dufferin, wasn't very far from the Italian sections of the city.

Deciding to take a friendly tone with him for once, Marie asked him bluntly why he didn't like her.

"I've been talking to my lawyer, Miss," Carlo said in a cheeky voice. "He says, you know, that teachers can't hit a poor defenceless student. He says he knows a teach, you know, who was sued for doing that. There are rules, you know."

"Cut that out, Carlo," she spoke sharply. "You've been rude and impertinent toward me all term. You're not that way ordinarily and I want to know why. You know, I can send you to the principal a third time. Why are you behaving so stupidly? You don't want to be expelled just because of me, do you?"

"You know, my lawyer will have something to say about that."

Feeling the anger rise in her, she looked down at her desk blotter and checked herself in time. Wrath and punishment seemed only to have stiffened him more against her.

"Listen, Carlo," she said, tired of her hard invincible pose. "I'm sorry about hitting you, but you've been absolutely obnoxious in my class all term. I could've thrown you out permanently months ago, you know. I'm asking you why you've been behaving as you have. Why don't you like me? What have I ever done to you?"

The emotion in her words seemed to get through to him. He looked down on the desk top, silenced out of his flippancy, his face showing some repentance.

"I don't know, Miss," he said. "It's you who doesn't like me."

"What makes you say that?"

"You know, Miss, you're the one who hit me."

"You provoked me, Carlo. Don't deny it. Why do you say I don't like you?"

He made a face, as if he had been given a ridiculous chore to perform.

"Remember at the beginning of term when you were

explaining, you know, about math? About how people think in a mathematical way?"

"Yes, I remember," she said, puzzled.

"Well, Mrs. Charlton, you said Italians, they didn't have, you know, a mathematical mind."

She was beginning to see what he was getting at.

"I was only joking, Carlo."

"It didn't sound like a joke to me. And then I hear these things about you, Mrs. Charlton. That you don't like Italians."

"Where did you hear that?" she said, feeling her voice quaver.

"From your students, you know."

"That's crazy, Carlo. Why would I dislike Italians? I'm an Italian myself."

His mouth hung open for a while.

"Gee, Mrs. Charlton, I didn't know that. You don't sound or look Italian at all."

"Well, my maiden name is Barone," she said, pronouncing the "e".

It turned out that Carlo's father, who worked at the Italian radio station, had instilled in his son a good amount of pride in their Italian heritage. Carlo was only defending the "honour of our ancestors", he said jokingly, but with some bite to his voice. He would do better to honour their memory, she said, by upgrading his poor marks and disproving her contention.

"If you could get a mathematical mind, Mrs. Barone," he said, "then I can too."

Later, as she was driving home to pick up Michael, it occurred to her that she knew very little of the Italian community in Toronto, except that it was fairly large—with close to half a million people—and had its own radio station and newspaper. During her interview with the principal a couple of years back, her Italian background had definitely proved instrumental in getting her the job. Richard hadn't been able to land his teaching job yet with the university and they desperately needed funds, so she had to use everything at her disposal. She had thought nothing of playing up the fact that she had been raised in an Italian neighbourhood by simple old-world parents. She would be teaching mathematics, after all, not sociology. But something the principal had said came back to mind: "You don't only teach the student, you teach the parents as well."

Marie, however, had used mathematics as a way of breaking her parental connection. To think mathematically, to think logically, was the only way to think independently and thus develop a mind of one's own. She not only taught algebra and calculus; she also tried to instil some grasp of the theory behind all the apparently mechanical procedures. That behind all the symbols and numbers and maxims lay the analytical method, the way of thinking, which was the most powerful tool to understanding and controlling the universe. And that this totally impersonal tool made them rise above such divisive things as language and background and emotion to achieve mastery over their own fate.

She hadn't realized that such thinking had given her a reputation for disliking Italians. It surprised and irritated her to have her comments so badly misunderstood. The thought of the principal hearing such things embarrassed her.

When she arrived at the daycare, the supervisor told her Michael had been cranky all day, refusing to participate in the games and behaving badly.

"What's the matter, Mikey?" she said, as her four-year-old son clutched at her skirt.

Michael was an odd little creature, given to extreme fluctuating moods. He could be withdrawn and sullen one moment and then highly boisterous and unmanageable the next. He had his father's fair hair and light complexion, but his eyes were unmistakably hers—with an even mixture of defiance and vulnerability fighting for control.

For all his education and progressive theories, Richard was

extremely conventional about the rearing of children. He blamed Michael's instability on the fact that she left him in a daycare all day, an accusation which, besides being highly unfair, hurt her very much. Probably because her husband had taken care of Michael the first few years she started working, he had developed a sharply critical attitude to the way she was rearing him. Nothing she ever did was "right". If she neglected him ever so little, that wasn't right. If she showed him a little too much attention, that wasn't right either. Richard believed in the correct proportion, a rather vague term that only he seemed to know the meaning of.

Marie suspected that Richard's overly fastidious concern for Michael sprang from more than the two years he cared for the child. Richard's parents had divorced when he was twelve, an occurrence that he spoke of lightly now but that seemed to have affected him more than he cared to admit. It was then, he said, he had first discovered that "the chicken came before the egg". What people demonstrably did, he said, proved what they were inside. You were loving because you did something loving, and not because you simply said or thought you were. The world as manifested and whole came before any theory and part. In layman's terms, he was fond of telling her, with dancing mischievous eyes, the chicken always makes the egg—not the other way around.

Well, she thought as she put Michael in the car, the chicken had certainly made this egg, and she had paid dearly for it.

As expected, they had married as soon as Richard had received his doctorate. A simple ceremony in an Anglican chapel at the University, which was attended by a few school friends. She wasn't overly bothered by her mother's absence, although she appreciated very much Joey and her father coming down. Although Richard didn't have a job yet, having the weight of his thesis removed from his shoulders suddenly made him carefree. He suggested they should have a child right away. She objected. She was still only in the initial stages of her own work. There was no telling how disruptive a child would be at that point. But he insisted. There would undoubtedly be a position open for him soon at the university. His doctoral supervisor was one of the most respected names there and had an international reputation in empirical philosophy. With his backing there was no worry. It was just a matter of time. It would only mean a couple of months or so away from her work. She finally gave in. Richard could be very persuasive when he set his mind to it.

Her health improved somewhat over the years. At least her weight remained stable. She was still shockingly thin and had the occasional days when she could scarcely eat a thing—but overall Richard seemed to steady her enough that her appetite didn't betray her as much as before. The doctors had diagnosed a mild form of anorexia nervosa, nothing to be overly worried about as long as she used her common sense. As her pregnancy advanced, however, she found herself eating more than ever. The doctor had advised her to gain weight or she would find it difficult to support the weight of the child. Besides, she couldn't think only of herself anymore. The child required nutrition too. By the time she was six months pregnant she started to miss classes and postpone appointments. She felt too bloated with food and Michael to face people. It became difficult to concentrate on her work. It seemed her body had taken command of her mind and refused it the least amount of energy to keep working. And when Michael was born, the terror of the delivery almost killing her, she was so overcome with the sheer living phenomenon of him that she lost all interest in her doctoral program.

For a while she and Richard were both delighted with what they had done. But then her husband wasn't able to obtain a position as quickly as he thought. She was forced to go to teachers' college and teach high school, her plans for a doctorate postponed indefinitely, and perhaps forever.

Now it seemed her husband wanted to deny her the opportunity of even having a job. Though teaching high school was a step down for her, she did enjoy being out and contributing something with her education. She hadn't gone to school for eighteen years and acquired a Masters to simply sit home all day dandling a baby on her knee.

Looking at the little boy sitting glumly in the car, however, Marie had a sudden pang of fear that perhaps her neglect of him at this point in his life would do him irreparable harm.

Marie parked the second-hand Toyota in the driveway and took Michael by the hand. They lived on the first two floors of an old three-storey house in the Annex, within walking distance of the Robarts Library, which Richard still used extensively, even though he was lecturing at a suburban division of the university. Richard had appropriated one of the three bedrooms for his study. The second served as the master bedroom, while the third was both her study and Michael's nursery. A couple of students occupied the third floor.

As soon as they got inside Marie took out Michael's toy box in the nursery and played with him.

"Let's play trucks, Mikey," she said, rolling a little plastic truck toward him.

He was refusing to speak to her, his face in an exaggerated pout. The truck hit him in the knee and rolled away.

Marie placed him on top of the four-wheeled plastic elephant and pushed him around the room. It seemed he was submitting himself to an ordeal. His eyes said: you can make me play with you, but you can't make me enjoy it.

"C'mon, Mikey, give me a break. Want me to read you a story, uh...?"

Looking into his eyes she saw he was a different human being from her—and capable of spurning her. He had come of her flesh and yet he had the capacity to think and feel in a way entirely different from her.

The revelation made her suddenly angry, as if he had absolutely no right to such a privilege. She had made him, carried him inside her, and now he had no right to be different from her. It was inconceivable that someone so much a part of her could do such a thing.

She read to him from a storybook about a fabled island where animals ruled over people and kept them as household pets. After a while Michael started to hum like a fighter plane. He spread his arms out and flew around the room. Snapping the book shut, Marie let out a tired sigh.

"All right, young man, wait till your father gets home."

Later when they were seated at the dinner table Marie found she had lost her appetite. She had made meat and vegetables for the others and an eggplant for herself.

Richard looked at her with practised concern. "How much have you eaten today? You're getting dangerously thin again."

The years had been rather good to him. His face had filled out well. He looked mature, distinguished—a man of means and purpose. Instead of wearing a beard, he had taken to combing his hair straight back, giving him a severe imperious bearing. Since getting the lectureship at the university he carried himself with the air of a man who had a sense of mission. He knew what he was about—and his peers had recognized his talents. He spoke regularly now of getting something published soon, of something that would set the academic community back on its ears.

However, along with his success had come an overbearing arrogance that she found hard to stomach. He often made disparaging remarks about her job and treated her condescendingly. She was no longer a fellow student aiming for the same things he was. She was a wife and mother now—a mere woman who had to fulfil her biological requirements.

It had been all right when she had first started working, but now that he had "his work" which overshadowed hers in every way, she had to fight constantly to keep some measure of self-respect. In some ways, in spite of all his education, it was the same sort of struggle she had conducted with her mother.

Dismissing the question with a sour expression, she told him about Michael's conduct.

"He's been a bad boy," she looked at her son disapprovingly. With a rebellious pout on his face Michael was squashing his vegetables into paste.

"Michael's just a little temperamental," Richard said. "Aren't you, Michael?"

His tone was patronizing, siding with her son against her. She knew that if she allowed Richard to have his way with the boy he would spoil him. He indulged him horribly, buying him all sorts of toys and listening to his every whim as if it were a desperate plea for love. "Patience and affection," her husband would say, "work better than anything. Children's feelings are the most delicate mechanisms." Richard seemed to treat the boy as a grown-up at times, speaking to him as if he understood the logic of good conduct like a college student.

"He's not temperamental," she said. "He's bad. Judy at the daycare said at first he wouldn't play with the other children and sulked in the corner. Then when he came over he threw mud at them."

"Marie, I've told you not to talk as if the boy weren't here."

She glared at her husband.

Concentrating on his food, he continued: "Maybe Michael wouldn't be so temperamental if his mother stayed with him a little more."

Marie looked crossly at her son. "Michael, you're supposed to eat them, not play with them."

"It's bad manners to play with your food, son," Richard said.

Michael continued playing with his food, not even bothering to look up.

"Eat your food, I said," she told him, her patience wearing thin. She could take just so much from both of them.

Michael looked up to his father, his face all hurt and innocence.

"I'm not hungry."

She snapped at him. "Young man, I told you to eat your

supper!"

"No, I won't. I'm not hungry."

The curt, open refusal struck a deep chord that unleashed an instinctive reaction. She reached over and cuffed the boy viciously on the back of the head. She was as much surprised as Richard, whose eyes registered shocked disbelief. Michael started to bawl uncontrollably. No-one moved.

Marie felt her body trembling. She couldn't bear to hear her son crying. He had become a separate person, capable of emotions and a life totally different from hers. Somehow that inescapable fact produced such an outpouring of hate toward him that some deep-seated fear had been uprooted.

Unable to stand it any longer, she ran to the bedroom, closed the door and fell crying on the bed.

By the time Richard came in she had gone through all the possible explanations for her unusual behavior. She wasn't eating very much and easily prone to being on edge. Her job was affecting her home life. Richard was insufferable, letting her do all the dirty work with Michael. Her body was betraying her again. But none of them satisfied her. It seemed she couldn't account for her actions at times.

Richard didn't waste any time in admonishing her. He couldn't believe she would revert to such barbaric methods of discipline. He thought she was enlightened, he said, with at least a modicum of good sense. Instead she was acting like a common fishwife.

"Is that all you can show from your Italian heritage?" he said sarcastically.

Marie looked at him, bewildered by the cold fury of his language. She felt she was in the wrong, but he had no right to tear into her like this.

"And how can you expect him to eat," Richard continued, "when you don't eat yourself? Don't you see what you're doing? What kind of example is that? Tell me."

She tried to defend herself, but her voice sounded no better than a whimper. "He has to eat. You can't just coax him anymore. He's a different person."

She was sitting cross-legged on the bed, with a ball of Kleenex in her hand, trying to understand what a different person was.

"Yes, he's different," Richard said, "and that's why you have to respect his wishes, listen to his reasons, try to understand what's going on inside."

"He's only four years old, for God's sake."

"Have you ever hit him before?"

"No."

"Well, don't do it again."

"He's not an adult, you know," she said indignantly. "He's a little boy who's stubborn and cranky at times. And he won't listen to reason."

"He has to see it demonstrated by good example first," Richard emphasized, as if he were closing the lid on the argument. "You're getting more muddled in your thinking than I thought. The words only verify the action. The words by themselves are nothing, the mere expression of a will that could be entirely divorced from reality."

His philosopher's tone stung her. Each time he used it she was reminded of her failure. He had ascended to the ranks, she had descended. It was a weapon he used on her, sharp and searing, which cut through to the bone. And the irony of it was that she had given in to his will at a time when to do so was the furthest thing from reality. She had done it to make him happy, but she had reduced herself in the process. Had split in two. And now that other part of her was beginning to disconnect himself from her, making her only half complete —and she could lash out at her husband for failing to see it.

"What has thinking to do with it?" she said. "He did something wrong. It hurts me to hit him. You don't know. He has a will of his own. I love him too much to let him have a will of his own. That sounds stupid, but it's true. How can I explain it. It's how I feel. It's too complex."

She knew she sounded incoherent, that he could use whatever she said and untwist it to make her see how inconsistent or paradoxical or meaningless it all sounded—but she didn't care. She couldn't be as self-conscious as he was, always in control, always with a neat explanation that made sense. Some things just didn't make sense. They happened. She loved Michael more than anything—and yet at the time she hit him she had felt such a tremendous hatred for him.

True to form, Richard began to lecture her on love, picking apart her words. His predictability abruptly distanced him from her. She regarded him coldly. His self-control. His fine analytical mind. His distinguished and self-assured bearing. All the things she had admired five years ago.

She felt an overpowering need to hurt him, to put a large dent in that insufferable smugness.

Before he finished she stopped him and eyed him silently, a cold, deadly smirk playing on her face.

"...the words only verify the action," she imitated his pedantic tone. "The words can only be the expression of a will entirely divorced from reality."

"So?" he said, impatient to continue.

"So, I would check your words against your actions as far as love is concerned," she said icily.

She didn't have to go on. She saw the hurt travel across his face and dig into familiar territory. It was a subject he was so delicate about that no further words were needed to spell it out. After five years of marriage they were attuned to the slightest reference to their faults and inadequacies.

Richard slumped down on the dresser chair, momentarily defeated.

Marie went to the nursery to check on Michael. He was sitting in the middle of his toys, talking out loud to keep himself company. As soon as he saw her his face lit up.

"Momma, you wanna play?"

He was hers again, she thought. He seemed to have completely forgotten the slap. The resiliency of kids amazed her. Grown-ups could hold grudges and resentments for decades, while kids lived in a less sinful world.

She picked him up and hugged him fiercely. "Momma's sorry, Mikey."

"Wanna play?" he repeated, disregarding the apology and wanting to get down to business.

Rolling the trucks across the carpet brought to mind the time she was his age. She could remember playing House with little teacups and running about in the fields around the tracks. She was hardly in the house. There was always something to do. Skipping rope. Playing hide-and-seek. Picking flowers. She hadn't been afraid to go after pollywogs with the boys either, or chase butterflies whose powdery wings stained your hands as they squirmed for life. The fields were full of flowers—buttercups and daisies and columbines and blue flags and forget-me-nots. She only learned their names afterward, of course, when they'd go on field trips from school—but she liked to walk among them when she was younger and look into their petals and watch the bugs crawling around and see how the colours were so true and beautiful.

How far the West End seemed to her now!

Richard had gone back with her for a few Christmases. Everyone had been overly polite and stiff, her mother unusually quiet at the dinner table as if she were intimidated by Richard's presence. She hadn't even prompted anyone to eat more. Marie had managed to get through the visits without any scenes. She ate only what she could, usually some salad and vegetables that she prepared on her own. Neither of them tried to make peace overtures. Assunta's sullen glances told her there was still much resentment to overcome.

Marie had only learned from her father how much Assunta had been hurt by her marriage ceremony in a Protestant chapel. "You know your mother, Maria," he said. "She wanted you to be married in the Italian way. In a church with a priest and a big reception so all her friends could come and see how good her daughter married." Looking down shyly at the floor, he shook his head. "I too would've liked to see that,

Maria." His words were so full of emotion that for the first time she saw the enormous repercussions of her action. She had broken something that perhaps could never be repaired.

"But, Babbo," she tried to explain. "Richard's not Catholic and I haven't gone to church in ages. It would've been a blasphemy. The priest wouldn't have allowed it."

But her father shook his head wearily. "Maria, we've lived in this parish for a long time. This priest knows you. He knows your mother very well. You're still part of the parish. Just because you live away...God knows how much your mother has put in the donation box all these years. And I did the priest a favour a long time ago. Do you see what I mean?"

"Maybe my next marriage, Babbo," she joked—but her father hadn't betrayed the slightest hint of a smile.

A couple of months after Michael was born her father had driven down to see the baby and asked her if she could make an unscheduled visit to the Sault.

"For your mother, Maria," he said.

"Tell her to come down herself," she told him peevishly. "She hasn't even seen where I've lived all these years."

But she relented a few months afterwards and brought the baby up by plane. Assunta had been reserved with the child in her presence. But on the second day of the visit her father had persuaded her to spend a day at the beach with Joey so that Assunta could take care of the baby alone. Marie had demanded a promise that her instructions for feeding the child would be scrupulously followed. When she came back in the evening she found Michael sleeping soundly on her parents' bed. There were all sorts of gifts and cards scattered around him on the bed and a baby carriage at the side.

"What's this?" Marie asked her mother who was beaming proudly.

"*È una sorpresa*—a surprise," she said.

But Marie immediately took the baby and said in Italian, "You have a shower without me, hey."

Her mother's face changed instantly. They spoke very little

after that. Her father was angry at her afterward.

"You spoil it, Maria," he said. "You spoil one of your mother's happiest days. What kind of a daughter are you, uh?"

"Who's the mother of this baby?" she said, still infuriated by her exclusion from the shower. "Tell me. Who?"

"And who's the *nonna*?" he said.

She had been less possessive in the subsequent visits, letting Assunta take care of Michael whenever she wanted. Her mother called him *Michele* and spoke Italian to him as if he understood it in his blood. But the visits were short and few and far between. Michael only spoke of his *nonna* before Christmas when he had an inkling that she would give him presents.

Later she gave Michael a bath and put him to bed. She continued reading the story of the animals and the witless humans. It ended with the humans rebelling against the tyranny of the animals and re-establishing their own rule.

"Things were the same as before," she read and closed the book.

The cynical ending didn't appeal to her at all. She was prepared to modify it for Michael's sake, but found him sleeping—probably long before he had heard the last details. She bent down and smelled the warm sweet aroma of her son.

How could her own child ever hate her, she thought.

She prepared her next day's lessons at her desk not far from Michael's bed. It was her favourite time of day, when she was alone in the company of the best part of herself. She lost any sense of inadequacy and failure—just felt deeply peaceful and strangely whole, felt that if she were to die right then, there wouldn't be any regrets.

Richard was already in bed reading when she finished. He usually worked well beyond midnight, then came in when she was asleep, and read until his feverish mind could be quelled.

"Sometimes," he told her once, "I think I've built a scaffold for myself that's like the tower of Babel...thinning out at the top, getting rickety and perilously dangerous as I go higher."

He hardly spoke to her of his work in any detail anymore. She suspected he felt her mind had turned to mush teaching adolescents, which wasn't far from the truth. She hadn't much time for keeping on top of her reading, what with Michael and all the kids at school to contend with. Besides, teaching students like Carlo made the job emotionally draining. It seemed to make the waters of her mind so turbid that she found it hard to see ideas clearly unless they were in front of her nose from over-familiarity or repetition.

"How's Michael?" Richard asked her in a conciliatory tone as she got into bed.

"Fine," she said curtly.

She was so exhausted that she immediately switched off the lamp on her side and turned her back to her husband.

After a moment of silence Richard persisted. "You shouldn't have hit him like that, Marie."

"Would you rather that he not eat at all then?"

"You know he'd get hungry eventually."

"Do I get hungry eventually?" she said, remembering that she hadn't eaten since her light lunch. "For food? For love?" She felt her eyes moistening.

"I do the best I can," he said.

"The best you can tells me you don't care for me anymore."

"That's not true. It's just my work is so demanding, Marie. Please understand."

"I understand," she said in a broken voice.

"Sometimes I get so excited by what I'm doing that physical things are...just not right."

"Which makes our marriage just not right," she told him.

It crossed her mind at that moment that one way Michael's birth had caused a radical change in her was that it was more and more difficult to deny the demands of her body. If Richard's work was pushing him higher into the sky, Michael's birth had brought her down, closer to the earth.

She could feel her body wanting to unravel, open up, and break through in the moist, dark earth. And that her body itself was composed of this moist, dark earth that wanted to take things in and push them out renewed and engorged with life. But these dark feelings made her feel guilty and afraid. She had for too long wanted to be like Richard, de-rooted and in control of herself, so that she could escape the West End.

It was all muddled, she couldn't help concluding. Things were so mysteriously connected. She couldn't separate them and see them clearly anymore. Things just happened.

It would humiliate her beyond measure to tell her husband she had to touch herself every so often. Because she couldn't be dry for too long. She had to feel that moisture in the dark, deep part of her.

"Is it that bad, Marie?" he said, touching her arm sympathetically.

Her tears were falling freely. But she couldn't tell him. She felt there was still something wrong inside her that she couldn't tell him.

"Marie, what's wrong?" he said, his voice imploring.

But her pain couldn't be translated into words. It felt tied in a knot in the pit of her stomach.

"Marie, please tell me."

She could only grit her teeth and endure it for however long it took.

"Marie...?"

Slowly she pulled away from him and turned her face into the pillow.

10

In the middle of May Joey had a long talk with Father Sarlo about his mother.

A week previously he had arranged an appointment with the family doctor, who had advised that the local psychiatrist be present.

"Don't worry, Joey," Dr. Contini said. "We won't let her know. She'll just think he's another doctor helping me out."

Dr. Contini was in his mid-thirties, with puffy cheeks and a thick waist. Joey was surprised to discover that he knew very little Italian. The city's two Italian doctors had died a while back, leaving the area open for the handful of second-generation young men who had come back to practise in their hometown. The doctor had asked Joey to come into his office to act as interpreter in case they needed him. The psychiatrist was a thin wan-looking man of British descent.

But once Assunta had an inkling of what was going on she stiffened and became unco-operative.

"I don't need this," she said, looking betrayed. "I go home."

"Ma, we're just talking," Joey said. "There's nothing wrong in talking."

"*Sei pazzo*—you're crazy."

Dr. Contini smiled. "This is for your good, Mrs. Barone," he said in textbook Italian.

"Ask her," the psychiatrist said, looking at Joey, "if she thinks she hasn't been doing anything out of the ordinary."

Joey took a deep breath before translating.

"Ma, do you think everything has been all right for you?"

She rolled her eyes, as if he had asked her the silliest question in the world.

"*Ma, che cosa,*" she raised her hand in the Italian gesture of contempt. "You crazy?"

Then turning to her doctor, she said plaintively, "*Dottore,* just give me a prescription and everything be all right. So I can sleep at night."

After this was translated for the benefit of the psychiatrist, Dr. Contini leaned toward his colleague and whispered a few things in his ear.

The psychiatrist was looking impassively at Assunta. "Ask her what she was doing on the train tracks at two in the morning."

"Ma," Joey said, now feeling like a ball being kicked around by both sides, "do you remember the time I met you on the tracks? They want to know what you were doing there."

She turned her eyes up again at the preposterous question.

"What do you think?" she raised her voice, her face as animated as he had ever seen it since the funeral.

Joey shrugged his shoulders and looked at the floor.

"What do you think?" she repeated, her voice high-pitched and defiant.

Joey looked up at her sheepishly. He noticed how her face had become more shrivelled and lean than ever. Her kerchief, tied tightly in a knot under her chin, seemed to be keeping the whole thing together. But her eyes were blazing indignantly. She gave the appearance at that moment not of his mother but of a proud and defiant old woman guarding herself from treachery.

Later they asked her all sorts of personal questions that he had never dared to ask himself. When she got tired of warding them off she simply refused to answer, sitting there with her ears turned off, although Dr. Contini's prescription to help her sleep seemed to appease her somewhat.

When Joey was speaking privately with the psychiatrist he apologized for his mother.

"We can't be of much help," the psychiatrist said, "unless your mother co-operates. She's a very stubborn lady. This method only works if the patient follows the rules. In the case of your mother, I'm not even sure she knows any of the rules."

"But what can I do?" Joey said, seeing the possibilities

dwindling hopelessly.

"We can set up a series of appointments, but I'm not sure they'll be worth the time. We've done some work with older Italian women, you see. They're very distrustful of people peering into their personal lives. Especially if they're religious. It's a job for the priest, you see. Not a psychiatrist. They have their own ways."

"She says she wants to go back to Italy."

"Yes, that's a natural request. Don't be too alarmed by it, though, if it's out of the question. She's probably using it more as a threat than anything else. To ensure attention. Tell me, is she a religious person?"

Joey nodded.

"Have her speak with her parish priest then. Explain what's happening to him. He'll probably be able to do better than we can. If the patient doesn't know the rules, you see, then there's no game."

Joey hadn't liked the cynical and, what seemed to him, dismissive attitude of the psychiatrist. And he had been too timid to ask if he thought his mother was becoming deranged in some way.

But in Father Sarlo's rectory at Our Lady of Mount Carmel he asked the old priest right off if his mother could be going insane. Although he hadn't been to church in over ten years he felt more comfortable in the rectory than in the doctor's office. They were sitting on cheap sofas in a small lounge area beside the office where the priest kept all the registers and papers of the parish.

"Not insane, Joey," the old priest said. "Just maybe a little confused."

They went on to talk about her behavior after Adamo's death. Father Sarlo mentioned how she sat in the same pew every morning in church. The way she always lit a candle after Mass.

"For my father?" Joey said, surprised.

The priest just looked at him.

"But they were always fighting. And they didn't show any affection toward each other. My sister always said they couldn't stand each other."

The old priest shook his head. "You young people, I don't know...."

Joey watched him closely as he talked. Except for Adamo's funeral, the last time he'd been this close to Father Sarlo was the last time he received communion, so long ago he couldn't remember. When the Italian priest was first transferred to the parish he was the scourge of the neighbourhood, railing against sin and stinginess with a fierceness Joey had never seen in a human being then or since. He had been mortally afraid of him. Of his indomitable figure—with his large flashing eyes behind the thick glasses and his long raven hair combed severely back. Of his occasional rages during which he'd spit his words out like a man possessed. Of the power of his office, which he used with such effect that Joey had often felt literally damned to hell.

Having gone to a seminary in Naples and assisted a couple of parish priests in Calabria, Father Sarlo had ruled Mount Carmel with an iron hand. Before he arrived the church had fallen into disrepair. The rectory was but a small house separated from the church. In a matter of a few years and through much ranting and raving he had managed to get enough funds from the parishioners to renovate the church from top to bottom and to build a new rectory. The priest's quarters and offices was a large brick attachment to the church. When it had first been completed and opened to the public, Joey could remember his father speaking of it disparagingly as a mansion more luxurious than any working man could dream of.

As Joey observed the cheap furniture and the threadbare linoleum he wondered at his father's remarks.

The priest seemed but a shell of his former self. All the hard lines in his face had collapsed. His hair was a fluffy white. And his eyes behind the bifocals were now subdued and sad.

He gave the appearance of a gruff old man who knew he had outlived his usefulness and was slightly bewildered at all the changes around him.

"I don't know," he kept shaking his head. "You judge love and affection in your own way. You see all this stuff in the movies and on TV. I don't know. I don't know what to think, my son. In the old country I used to see marriages where the wife and husband hardly talked to each other—but if you took away the husband or took away the wife, the other became nothing. In small villages and farms where they worked all day, love meant living with a person for many years. Love came from a need. How can I tell you, Joey? It's like bread. You need bread to live. Then from your need you come to love your food. Well, in these poor areas you couldn't do all the work alone. You needed a partner. Then you needed children. It was simply the fulfillment of these needs. But over here, I don't know. It's all different." The old priest shook his head vigorously.

"And when a husband died," he continued, "there were certain customs for the *vedova*—the widow—some very harsh and merciless customs, let me tell you. In these villages everyone watched that the widow observed the customs closely. The husband died but she had to keep his memory alive—and also his honour. She had to deny herself many things. She couldn't go to a festa, or a wedding or a christening. Nor even to the piazza. Because she couldn't really be seen in public during daylight. She had to depend on the neighbours for food. And each day she had to set aside a certain time for public wailing in her home. So her fate was very much linked with that of her husband. In our village in Calabria we had a saying: when the husband died the wife got the worst of it." The priest looked at him sadly. Joey had to turn his eyes away.

He thought over the priest's words for a minute.

"But no-one around here does that sort of thing anymore, Father."

"Yes, but there are times when the traditions are strong and can't be easily controlled."

"Can you speak to her, Father?"

The priest cast a shifty glance at him.

"Sure, I can speak to her, but it's you who's the stranger to this church. She has her faith. She's lived her life. I don't see much wrong with her."

"But she walks the tracks at two in the morning," Joey insisted.

"Yes, and she goes to Mass every morning, too," the priest smiled cryptically. "Isn't that very odd for her too?"

"Father, you know what I mean. Will you speak to her? Find out what's happening? I don't know what to do."

"I speak to her through the Mass every morning, my son. Why can't you speak to her?"

"I don't know the language as well as you do. I don't understand what she's doing. Since my father's death it's like she's become a total stranger. I've lost touch with her, Father."

"You young people," the old priest said, his voice regaining some of the sharp edge of the pulpit. "You should be ashamed of yourselves. You grow up in this community, in an Italian home with good parents who work to the bone for you, and what do you do? You grow away from your mother tongue. You lose your culture and your heritage. And then you become strangers with your parents. They come to this country mainly for you, so that you can have the advantages denied to them—and what do you do? The first moment you get the opportunity you turn your back to them."

"But I stayed here, Father," Joey protested.

"I'm not talking mainly of you, my son. But all the others who left. All the others..."

The priest looked abstractedly around him. Joey thought for a moment he was trying to locate his parishioners in the church.

"I see the old people come to Mass now," Father Sarlo continued, "and I see it in their eyes. They come from the old-age homes here, or from the ones across the city. No matter where they've moved to they come back to this church, to something that's familiar, that's part of them. It's their home. It's where their children were baptized and had their first communion. It's where they want their children to be married. I've had parents begging me to marry sons and daughters who have moved as far away as Texas. Marry my daughter, Father, they say. She lives far away, but she was raised in this church. I know, Joey. Believe me, I know how far the sons and daughters have scattered from this neighbourhood. I see it in the eyes of the old people. What you have to know about these people, Joey," the priest leaned closer, filling the air with his fetid breath, "is that they come from places—villages and towns—where their families had lived for generations. Coming to this country was like going to the ends of the earth for them. Like going to China."

There was still enough power in the priest's words to scare him. Even if Joey had wanted to interrupt him he knew he couldn't. Many of his childhood fears and nightmares were wrapped up in that old black cassock.

"They needed this neighbourhood," the priest said. "It was the place in between China and the old world. Where they could make a place like home. Like a village where everyone could know each other and where there was a sense of community. I remember when we had to renovate this church. Everyone pitched in, made sacrifices, because a village is nothing without the house of God. Something that would make them proud of themselves. Even your father, Joey, who wasn't a religious man, he worked on the church. He was a builder and he knew he had to pitch in his share for the neighbourhood. It was his job. And it was my job to see that he knew what his job was—even if he thought he'd never use what he built."

The old priest smiled for a moment, as if recollecting a funny incident between him and Adamo.

"Your father and the others, Joey, they helped build this

neighbourhood. Now they're almost all gone. There are so many different people moving into these apartment buildings. It's hard for me to keep up. Maybe it's good they're sending in a replacement for me, uh? An Irish priest in the West End! Have you ever heard such a thing?"

Despite his reproaches, Father Sarlo arranged for Assunta to come and see him every day after Mass. Soon after, her walks on the tracks stopped altogether. When asked about her meetings with the priest she only said, "We talk about the old country—and sometimes about you and Marie."

Joey also discovered that Father Sarlo had requested to be sent back to Italy, to his birthplace—a village in the Calabrian hills—where he'd live in semi-retirement.

At first the news disquieted him. It was possible that the old priest was building up expectations for Assunta that had no way of being realized. But when he gave it further thought, it didn't seem such a preposterous idea after all. His mother had requested to be sent back enough times. And there was always Pia who would take care of her in Novilara. The only problem, as he saw it, was that he couldn't take his mother's request too seriously. She had been away too long from the old country. Her family, at least what was left of it, was here. Something kept telling him that she didn't really want to go back, that she really didn't want her words to be taken at their face value.

Mentioning this to Marie on the phone the Sunday after his talk with Father Sarlo, he asked if Assunta's request could be genuine or not.

"I don't see why not," Marie said. "That's where she's always belonged, isn't it? Her parents probably forced her to come here and marry Dad. At any rate, she's never adapted. She's stayed adamantly Italian. Probably without knowing any better either. Which hasn't made it any easier for us, you know."

"What do you mean?"

"Look at yourself, Joey," she assumed her pedantic tone.

"Have you ever asked yourself why you've stayed so long in that house? Why you didn't leave to play hockey? Or why you're not settled down and married yet?"

"C'mon, Marie," he said, annoyed whenever she tried to delve into his personal life and offer her miraculous solutions.

"It's because she's kept you in that house as an emotional cripple. She's done everything for you like a true Italian Mamma, hasn't she? Cooked for you. Washed, ironed... scraped you clean. All you have to do is bring home a paycheque. And be fairly content and appreciative of all she's ever done for you. Has she ever thrown you out and made you meet people...girls, I mean? Has she ever encouraged you to settle down and get married? Have you ever asked yourself why?"

"C'mon...."

"Because that house is the extent of her world, like a castle surrounded by the moat of the West End. And she's always needed her men to safeguard her from attack. Now I see why I was never valued as you men. She knew I wouldn't be able to safeguard her castle."

"Well, *no-one* can anymore," he said dejectedly. "The house has been sold and we have to move out by the end of the summer."

There had been no way to delay the planners any longer. Once he told them he was prepared to sell, they pressured him into signing the papers as quickly as possible. It was done: he had sold the house his father built.

The bit of news seemed to stop Marie short. They stayed silent for a while.

"Have you told her yet?" Marie asked, her voice anxious and entirely stripped of its teacher's tone.

"No, but I think she's suspected it would happen ever since the widow Angeline sold her place."

"Joey...?"

"Yeah?"

"I want you to tell her the right way."

"You don't think she really wants to go back to Italy, then, do you?"

"Yes, I do, but the decision has to be hers. Do you know what I mean, Joey?"

"But she wants to go."

"You can't tell her about the house yet, Joey. Understand?"

He was afraid for a few days afterwards that this new development would change Marie's plans for coming back. So he called her again and asked her.

"Don't worry," she said, "I've already sent in my letter of resignation."

Relieved, he said, "At least she's not walking the tracks anymore. She hasn't said much, but I think she's really looking forward to your arrival."

"You should know, Joey, that Richard has been wanting to see me again. We both love Michael too much to let him go much longer without having a father. Our differences aren't important enough to put Michael's future in jeopardy. So I'll come up for the summer. But after that I'm not sure. Especially if Mom is going back to Italy. I thought maybe I might finish my doctorate back here."

The news upset him for a moment.

"As long as you come back at the end of June like you said."

He made it sound as threatening as possible. He had a life of his own as well. Especially now that Annalise was occupying so much of his time.

Somehow her hockey sketches, combined with her gradual recovery of health, had sparked a renewed interest in work. "I seem to know what I should paint now," she said. In a sudden burst of energy she had rented a room for a studio above a downtown store. Neither the art room at the high school nor her basement had worked out. Joey had helped her clean the place and transfer her stuff there. It was spacious and well lighted, with a high enough ceiling and large windows overlooking the street and the river further south. He had gone over to help her make frames at first, surprised at how much wood was required for her huge canvases. Then he found she needed shelves and work benches, so he had brought some of his father's tools over and started work on those. From helping his father work on the house all those years he discovered he had acquired a certain talent for carpentry. The grain of wood felt familiar and good in his hands. It gave him great satisfaction to cut, plane, and contour the wood to make something useful for Annalise. He enjoyed being in the same room with her while she applied herself to her work with a tenacity and absorption that made him envious. At times she was able to work non-stop from the early evening to three or four in the morning. There was a cot in the room in case she had to stay overnight. On more than one occasion he had stayed with her.

Just recently Annalise had radically changed her way of depicting her sketches of "Soo Life", as she called them. It was as if she had gone to the opposite extreme. Where before they were merely splashes of colour and totally unrecognizable, they were now highly representational, except that she tended to put things in the most unusual positions. One canvas she had just finished had hockey players enmeshed in goal nets as they were manoeuvring on the ice. And the colours were all switched around as well. Black for blue. Or yellow for white.

When he timidly asked her why she had changed she said, "I saw I was just being derivative, doing what New York was doing. I have to do the Sault. I can't do New York. I've never even lived there. I have to do the Sault the way I see it. You can't be anyone else but yourself. I used to believe content was nothing, form and colour everything. But now I see it's all malarky. There's no such thing as form and content. There's only what you see as you see it. I want to get out of the head and out of the self-consciousness. I want to have people see what they see as if for the first time. The marvel of it."

He hardly knew what she was saying, but her eyes were blazing and she had that flush in her face that made the meaning of her words irrelevant for him. It was Annalise vibrating with the sense of herself. It merely made him nod sheepishly. He could believe her because she wouldn't lie to him.

When Joey mentioned to Marie that he was bringing Annalise over to the house for the first time, his sister was silent for a minute. He had told her that he was serious about Annalise. Assunta used to tell them half-jokingly that they weren't to bring anyone home to dinner unless they were prepared to marry them.

"I'd like to be there to see that," Marie said. "But I'd be careful, if I were you, Joey. You know how Mom is. She has to get used to changes gradually."

Joey brought Annalise over to dinner on a Saturday in the first week of June. Annalise had worked in the morning, and then they had looked at apartments in the afternoon. Annalise was working on something she wouldn't show him. "A surprise," she said, smiling. She was clearly too good for him. He was often intimidated by her cleverness, the way she could summon up facts or concepts at will and articulate them with ease and assurance. "I can never keep up with you," he complained to her once. "Oh yes you can!" she had exclaimed, eyeing him with a raw candid hunger. It seemed she was insatiable. She lost herself completely when it came to making love.

"Don't expect too much from her," Joey told Annalise about his mother. "It's like she's in another world."

Except for avoiding the tracks there had been no change in Assunta's behavior since she had spoken to Father Sarlo. Like clockwork she went to church each day at seven. Then she made a hasty breakfast, took it up to the TV room, and turned on the TV. For the rest of the day, except for the times she needed to get more food or to stretch her legs, she sat immobile on the sofa, either watching the endless programs she could scarcely understand or dozing off. In retrospect, he saw that walking the tracks had at least provided some exercise she badly needed. Her prolonged immobility was sapping her strength badly. Each day he saw her movements becoming progressively slower.

The TV room had so much become her private lair that Joey found it hard to keep her company. She neglected to clean up after herself and there was always some form of garbage or leftover food lying around. The room smelled awful. He did what he could to clean things up, but she wouldn't let him touch anything when she was there, and shift work sometimes prevented him from being around for weeks at a time.

When they watched TV together their only form of conversation consisted of questions and answers about the program. Lately, however, she had stopped asking questions altogether. They'd sit in silence for hours. He found he could turn the channel selector at will without the slightest protest from her. It gave her an idea. She asked him to buy a remote-control selector so she wouldn't have to move all the time. She sat there afterward going from channel to channel until something caught her fancy. The whole thing was more than he could understand. It seemed she was mesmerized by the screen itself. It didn't matter what was on. In the afternoons she would go from one soap opera to the next without losing interest. When he tried to engage her in conversation she either answered in monosyllables or told him to be quiet.

"But, Mamma," he said, "you don't even understand what they're saying."

At which she regarded him with that particular stony glance that would silence him instantly.

He began to stay away from the TV room altogether. She didn't ask him about the nights he stayed with Annalise. He could have been working the night shift, for all she knew.

Bringing Annalise to the TV room, Joey introduced her to Assunta. Annalise said hello. His mother sat rigidly on the sofa, disregarding both of them.

"Mamma, you don't want to say hello?" he said in Italian.

Instead she proceeded to change the channels quickly. He

looked at the screen. By the position of the window light he could see his mother's face reflected off the screen. She was staring impassively back at him.

"It's all right, Joey," Annalise said. "We'll come back after and speak with her."

"Mamma, we're going down to eat dinner," he spoke as if to a child. "We'll bring something up for you, okay?"

He made the salad while Annalise prepared an omelet.

"Do you always eat in the basement?" she said. "Where's the green pepper?"

He showed her where the vegetables were. Assunta hadn't made a regular meal in six months. Some of the food had spoiled.

"It's an Italian custom here."

Annalise enjoyed cooking. She had become adept at it during her high school days when Nicole had gone back to work. "It's like an art," she said. She liked to make large elaborate omelets, which tasted fantastic.

"Is it also an Italian custom for a widow to do what your mother is doing?"

"The old priest here told me they had weird customs in the old country. But you saw her. She's gone too far. We don't know what to do with her."

"She's bound to snap out of it," she said reassuringly.

"I never thought she'd take it so hard."

He told Annalise about some of the things he had been afraid to tell her before. Of the way Assunta had cut her hair. Of walking the tracks. Of the visit with the psychiatrist.

"You should've seen her," he said, smiling, "Sitting there, moving her hands wildly, and telling us we were all crazy."

"So she's not always quiet like just now?"

"Oh no. There's a reason for that. But I'll tell you, my father's death has affected us in strange ways. With her it's sort of stopped her cold. With me it's pushed me forward... freed me in a way. I really don't know how to explain it."

"It's awakened you," she said. "Remember?"

"Yes. But more too. Because I can feel my father inside me somehow. I find myself sometimes doing what he'd do. Or I stop in the middle of an expression and it's his expression, you know. It's hard to explain. I feel free of something and yet my father seems to live more inside me than ever before."

He was shaking his head, perplexed by the paradox of it all. But he couldn't explain it any better. He just felt it deep inside him.

Annalise remained silent, intent upon her omelet. They were both at the counter, standing away from the table. Upstairs he could hear the TV droning on. At times he had the impression his mother was like some moth who was entranced by the glow of a lamp. Sometimes he became so sick of that noise he felt he could hurl a hammer through the screen.

"You know," he continued, "I haven't done anything with my life yet. I've felt so sorry for myself all these years. Working in the plant instead of playing professional hockey. Sleepwalking all the time. My father used to tell me I had to find a trade. Do something that defined my life. He was a bricklayer, he used to say. When they saw him, they saw a bricklayer. What can I be?"

He felt foolish talking like this, but Annalise seemed to bring things out of him. It was as if the words had always been there, but he had never had the opportunity to say them.

Annalise casually said, "What about a carpenter?"

"What about it?"

"You seem to have a flair for carpentry."

"C'mon. All I did was make a few shelves."

"I can see when someone is good with their hands, Joey. Don't be falsely modest. You'd have to apprentice yourself to someone, of course. There aren't too many people who make furniture by hand anymore. But my father knows a few who work on it as a sideline. What they make is very expensive and profitable, I'll tell you."

He laughed, not taking her seriously. "You paint and I make chairs, is that it?"

Turning around to put the salad on the table, Joey was startled to see his mother standing at the foot of the stairs staring at them. They had been so preoccupied that they hadn't heard her. Her face was tensed in an angry scowl.

"What you doing in my kitchen?" Assunta said harshly.

Joey thought she was joking and relaxed. "Nothing, Ma. Just making dinner. Do you want us to make you something?"

"Who told you to use my kitchen?" she said.

He looked at her more closely. She was deadly serious.

"Take it easy, Ma. We're only making dinner like we said. Is anything wrong?"

"You get out of my kitchen! Get out!"

Annalise said, "Let's go, Joey. She means it."

"Wait a minute." Joey took a few steps toward Assunta. He saw her body tremble with anger.

"Ma," he said, addressing her calmly. "You can't do this to my friend. We're not doing anything wrong. You just take it easy and go upstairs, okay. I'll come to talk to you in a few minutes."

He felt embarrassed in front of Annalise and anxious now to avoid a further scene. His mother must have been more unstable than he thought.

"No!" Assunta raised her voice. "This is my house. My kitchen. You no use my kitchen."

"Mamma, listen," Joey felt his temper rising. She had gone too far. "Please go upstairs. Stop this foolishness. It's disgraceful. I come up to talk to you later."

"No."

Assunta came into the kitchen as if Annalise wasn't there and proceeded to prepare her own meal. Annalise looked at him and stepped away. Assunta's black-garbed figure put their things away, as if she had taken possession of her domain again.

"It's all right, Joey," Annalise told him. "I'll wait in the car for you."

Joey waited for Annalise to get out of the house. He looked at Assunta, his blood rising. She tried to make as if nothing had happened. She was still in control of things. She was the mother of a twelve-year-old kid.

"This is *not* your house, Ma," he said, infuriated with her. He felt the need to make her see he wasn't to be treated so disrespectfully anymore. That he was a man in control of the situation now. That he wasn't that twelve-year-old kid anymore who spoke a twelve-year-old language.

She went to the fridge and took out some ricotta cheese.

"Did you hear me, Ma? This is not your house."

Assunta looked at him as if he were speaking like a fool.

For a moment he wanted so badly to explain to her, to tell her with the words he knew in English, how much Adamo's death had changed him. And bridge the gulf that separated their worlds with his feeling for her.

But it was no use. He would never be able to find the words.

The exasperation infuriated him even more. The look she gave him instinctively told him he couldn't get through to her with a twelve-year-old's language.

"What are you saying?" she said smugly. "This is my house."

"No, Mamma!' he had to shout back. "This is my house."

"*Stupido!*" she yelled back. "This is my house."

Losing his temper, he screamed at the top of his voice.

"It's my house, understand! Babbo left me this house! It's mine, not yours!"

It took her a few seconds to get the full import of his words. Her face looked perplexed. Betrayed.

"I sold this house, Mamma. It's sold, understand. The city owns it now. We have to move out by the end of the summer."

"*Giuseppino,* what're you saying?"

Her voice was so full of alarm it burned in his ears.

"It's not our house anymore." Suddenly he felt so spent he had to slump down on a chair. Assunta stood over him, her face stricken.

"You sold this house, Joey?" Through the window he could catch part of Annalise's head in the car. She was waiting patiently for him.

He explained as best he could that they had no choice in the matter. The city would have expropriated their property eventually.

Assunta's face looked crushed. She was taking short gasps of air as if her heart was failing her.

There was a long painful silence. He felt himself choking with the need to tell her how much she meant to him. How much he had hidden his love for her and Adamo in a stupid reticence that couldn't be excused by any differences in language or culture.

It was just a matter of getting up and putting his arms around her. It looked so easy. There was only a few inches of air between them. All he had to do was move his hand through those inches and touch her. Just as he was becoming accustomed to with Annalise.

But he couldn't do it. The space between them was still too large, even though it had dwindled appreciably in the past while.

Joey felt the next time he was sure to do it. He had come so close this time that he needed one more time to close the final gap.

"*Mi dispiace,* I'm sorry, Mamma," he said, "but you haven't been well the past few months. You knew it was only a matter of time. You shouldn't have treated Annalise like that. If you send her out of the house you send me out too."

Assunta sat down. She wouldn't look at him. She was crying silently.

"Mamma, Marie and I will send you to Italy, if you still want to go. You don't have to go if you don't want to. Think about it, okay. I have to drive Annalise home now. We'll talk some more when I get back."

On Wednesday of the following week Marie called. She was all excited, her voice spilling out the words so quickly he couldn't get a word in edgewise. He listened with a sinking heart.

"Joey, listen, I can't come up at the end of the month. Not just then, anyway. Richard and I have to straighten things out between us. We're going on a short vacation with Michael. It's important to me, to Michael, understand. We have to make things work out between us. There's no other way. Mom and Dad at least taught me that. Tell Mom I'll be up sometime in the summer. Don't worry about her. She's made of stone."

11

It had been a nightmare from which he could never recover. The memory of it would haunt him for the rest of his life.

At times he thought it should never have happened. He could have prevented it. Or foreseen it, at least. The warning signs had been clear enough. But perhaps only clear in hindsight, he thought. For he had been totally unprepared for the shock.

At other times he believed the events were beyond his control. He had done more than enough, he repeatedly told himself. How could he have stopped a force of nature or an accident? If indeed it was an accident.

Yet he could never hope to console himself completely. He had been entrusted with the care of a human being. And he had failed. There were no excuses in the long run. He should have watched out for her more carefully. He shouldn't have been so blinded by his own concerns.

And he couldn't completely exonerate Marie, either. Even though she had been 500 miles away. The callous timing of her change of plans seemed to be the final rebuff in a long list of misunderstandings.

The events of those few days were still as clear as ever in his mind. He had turned them over, sifted through them, balanced them repeatedly on his own scale of values—in order to make some sense of something that was a sorrow beyond his worst nightmares.

After Assunta had found out about the house she lapsed into a deep despondency. She refused to speak to him altogether. He felt she was punishing him unfairly. He made efforts to apologize, but she completely disregarded him. By the time Marie called to change her plans he was fed up with the whole thing. He had tried to do his best for the sake of the family—to keep it together if possible—and had only been abused in the process.

He told this to his sister. "All right, Marie, but it's about time you took some of the consequences. You're the oldest."

She said not to worry. She said their parents had lived their lives and now it was up to them to think of themselves first. To put their lives in order.

Assunta took Marie's change of plans with a blank face. It was as if she had expected nothing but the worst all along. Marie hadn't so much disappointed her as merely lived up to expectations.

Joey stayed with Annalise whole days at a time. He would only come home to change his clothes or pack his lunch. He was on day shift that week and would go straight to the studio and work at his carpentry until Annalise returned from school. Then they'd go out to eat, meet friends for a while, and come back to work the night. He felt he had discovered another world. Where one's work consumed every thought, every minute, of the day. He was, for that short period, living a few feet off the ground. His life seemed to matter like never before. The plant was where he went to sleep for eight hours.

He didn't feel he could sleep another eight. Somehow, making love to Annalise and the sense of making something on his own and their constant proximity all seemed to merge into an intensity of feeling that left him shaking with excitement. He was buzzing with something. Annalise said she had always known he was passionate. She took the credit for awakening him. She called him her Sleeping Beauty.

At the end of the week he decided to go home and have it out with his mother. He would apologize and make her see everything was all right. She wouldn't have to go to Italy. If she wanted she could live near the widow Angeline in the old-age home. Or if she wanted her own house, he'd buy her that. He'd visit her all the time. She'd get used to Annalise. They'd give her all the grandchildren she wanted. She'd have them coming out of her ears.

But when he got home her place was vacant. It was nine in the morning and she might have been still talking to Father Sarlo after Mass. He had a chance to clean up the TV room. He removed all the garbage, tidied up the magazines, fixed the sofa, and aired the room. It was strange to have the TV off. He looked at its dark malevolent screen. It was his enemy now.

By ten she hadn't returned yet. He phoned Father Sarlo at the rectory.

"We had a good long talk," the priest informed him. "Then I heard her confession and she left. That was an hour ago, Joey."

"Did she say where she was going?"

"Home."

"Did she sound all right?"

"A little depressed. But she feels she isn't allowed any better than that."

"What did you talk about?"

"You, my son. You've been neglecting her."

"I have a life of my own, Father."

"She's your Mamma, Joey. Don't forget that you're Italian."

"I know," he bowed his head.

"Don't worry. She's probably speaking to someone she's met along the way."

But everyone he called didn't know where she was. The only possibility was that she had gone to the fields. But even so, it wouldn't have taken her this long.

After another half-hour's wait he went out looking for her. Instead of going west to James Street he went by way of the tracks. It was the path she would have taken from the church. Something in Father Sarlo's voice hadn't been quite right. Or maybe it was just his imagination and the guilt he felt for having neglected her the past week.

He walked past Queen alongside the ties. There was no one on the tracks this time of day. It was bright and warm, with only a few clouds in the sky. The International bridge loomed just to his left. Its green huge girders swept away as far as the eye could see. He followed the line of the tracks. The swing-bridge over the Canadian locks broke the horizon. It was disconnected from the tracks and parallel to the locks. The farther he went the higher the elevation got. There wasn't a soul in sight. He stopped at the small truss bridge. It afforded him a good vantage point. He could remember panning over the horizon like a ship's captain. Over to the west and the steel plant, then turning counter-clockwise to the river and the locks, and finally to the paper mill on the east.

For some reason he had lost his sense of anxiety at that moment. He saw his boyhood playground for what it was. Unused and despoiled railroad land blanketed with over-grown grass and shrubbery.

He looked in every direction for the familiar sight of his mother stooping in the fields. With her apron full of dande-lions. Harvesting the one wild crop that reminded her of home. But he couldn't see her. He could remember distinctly the two thoughts that crossed his mind at that moment—that there must have been a lot of dreaming to make these fields seem like the land she had never wanted to leave and that, unlike dandelions, people couldn't be uprooted quite so easily.

So that when his eye caught the severed black shape of a human being in the ditch beside the track just below him it was as if he had seen the shattering of a dream.

The few minutes immediately afterward were lost forever. His mind had been clicked shut by the flick of a switch. But then the flashes of memory came back in all their sickening clarity. The rushing toward the body. Hurtling down the steep hill. Feeling the little coal and gravel stones wedging into his shoes. Stopping and falling on his knees. The final jolting recognition. The body sliced and mangled by the train. The vomiting. The sudden alterations between rage and total incomprehension. The deep primal scream inside him that never came out. Then the loss of speech altogether, so that when he called the police and ambulance he didn't recognize who was talking.

He was in a daze for hours afterward. But he had to go back with the police to the tracks. To show them where the body was. To explain what he thought had happened. How she must have been under the bridge after picking dandelions. How she must have not heard the train coming round the bend from the plant. Or she had lost consciousness somehow on the tracks. Or fallen and hurt herself. Because, just as surely as they were standing on firm ground, the train had sliced her in half.

During the phone call to Marie he found he couldn't put it into words. She had to guess from his incoherent and inarticulate whines. The rest of the day was lost going over every detail of the occurrences in self-inflicted punishment.

That night he called Annalise. But even she couldn't ease the pain. Midway through the night he persuaded her to sleep in Marie's room. He wanted to be alone.

Joey spent the rest of the night in the TV room, pacing in a tight circle, trying to calm himself. At one point he searched the room from top to bottom. When he didn't find anything he searched again. Instinctively he yearned for some scrap of information that would tell him exactly what had happened. Anything that would muzzle the hydra-headed questions that were tearing away at his flesh.

"Mamma," he said out loud. "What happened?"

But he found nothing. And he had the sickening thought that in dying she had forever shut the door on herself and thrown away the key.

The next day he picked Marie up at the airport. She was like a walking skeleton. She had lost even more weight since Adamo's funeral. Her face was so emaciated it had the sharpness of a hatchet. Her bare arms were like match sticks.

From the way she looked she could have been starving herself for weeks. Her skin was pale and sickly. Her eyes were red from crying. Along with the grief in them there was a strange lifelessness.

As they nodded in greeting Marie suddenly embraced him. He stiffened as he felt her bony cheek brush his neck.

"Oh, Joey, how could it have happened?" she said, breaking into tears.

He made no attempt to answer her. Standing there with all the people milling about the arrival room, he felt she was a complete stranger to him. He remembered only six months ago in that very room she had arrived for Adamo's funeral. It was like a replay of a sickening joke.

They were halfway to the city before she ventured to speak again.

"I'm sorry," she said, looking ahead of her.

"For what?" His voice was cold and bitter.

"I'm just sorry," she said.

Back at the house he told her he had already made the necessary phone calls.

Sardonically, he said, "The numbers were still fresh in my mind."

She gave him a perplexed look, but didn't dare say anything. After bringing her things to her room and freshening up, she didn't come back down immediately. He thought she was napping, or maybe avoiding him.

Joey went over what he would say to her. At the hospital he had told the police about the *cicoria* and how devout a churchgoer his mother was. Father Sarlo had been brought in to confirm his story. The priest also mentioned in passing that Assunta was recently widowed. Nothing was mentioned of her unstable behavior. Joey instinctively felt he had to protect her against public disclosure. He had realized what a mistake it was to bring her to a psychiatrist. If neither he nor the psychiatrist could penetrate through her behavior, he reasoned, how could others ever understand? He wouldn't betray her twice.

The police nevertheless said there would have to be an autopsy.

When Marie came down to the basement kitchen she was dressed in a fashionable black dress brazenly decorated with white flowers.

"It's the only black dress I have," she said by way of apology.

"It looks like a nightgown," he scoffed.

"I'm sorry," she turned away.

"Forget it. Do you want anything to eat?"

"What's there to drink?"

He went into the cantina to get a bottle of wine. He noticed it was five to seven. They'd be finished with the autopsy by the end of the night, they told him.

"Isn't there anything else?" Marie noticed the wine. "I've never liked the stuff."

"No," he said curtly.

He made himself some eggs while his sister poured the wine. He hadn't eaten anything substantial since the day before yesterday. It made him glad to see Marie grimace as she drank the wine. He noticed he had absent-mindedly taken his father's place at the table.

"Where's Michael?" he asked her.

"Staying with Richard."

"So, you're going to get back together again." His voice was mocking. Somehow he wasn't intimidated in the least by her anymore. Her education, her life in the big city, her superior airs amounted to nothing in the face of what had happened.

They were silent for a long while. He saw that she was getting used to the wine. It was strong and full-bodied. He had helped Adamo make wine in the autumn since he could remember. This coming season he'd have to make it alone. He'd order the dark California Marsala, put them in the press, and smell the pungent aroma of the squashed skins.

"Someone's been sleeping in my bed," Marie said.

"It's not your bed anymore, is it? You haven't lived in this house for over ten years."

He stared accusingly at her.

"What's wrong with you, Joey?" she said, put off by his manner for the first time.

Disregarding her question, he started to give the particulars of Assunta's death. Where the body lay. How he had found it. The way it looked. Sliced in half and mangled. The flesh and bones exposed like the side of an accordion. The blood over the ties and splattered on the black dress. Like a squashed bug.

"Stop!" she said, closing her eyes.

"I want to make you see it the way I saw it," he glared at her fiercely.

"Why are you so cruel, Joey?" She went to the fridge where the Kleenex was, the tears falling freely.

"Don't you know?" he said, shoving the plate away and gulping his wine.

"You blame me?" she said incredulously.

He abruptly got up, shaking the table. "You don't know?" he said, unable to face her at that moment. "You don't know?"

He poured himself another glass and started pacing back and forth.

"I can't believe this," Marie said. "I wasn't even here." She was crying and drinking at the same time.

"You don't know?" Joey said, almost inarticulate with suppressed rage. The wine felt dark and ominous in his stomach, stoking a violent eruption.

"I wasn't even here."

"Ah!" he shouted, as if she would see his point. He couldn't bring up the words. They were there, he could feel them, but they were all mixed up with the Italian words of his parents.

"What's wrong with you, Joey," she said. "What could I do? I don't even belong here. I have *never* belonged here."

"So you left, uh.... So you never came back, uh."

"I've always felt like a foreigner here, Joey. You've never known." She seemed to be speaking from some deep part of her that she had never exposed to him before.

Joey felt his body tremble.

"But she's your mother," his voice didn't sound his own. "You owed her something."

"She's never understood me. I could never get along with her."

"You should've stayed here. This is your home."

"I have my own life. She's never loved me."

He could have smashed her, so hard-headed she was. Like a stone statue turned to face one view all its days.

He shouted, "She had you in her belly...what are you talking about love!" The words spilled out involuntarily like vomit. "You should've been here taking care of her. You didn't have to speak to her. Just be here. Love!" he spat out the word as if it were poison. "You were looking for the wrong thing, *stupida!*"

And, abruptly, as if possessed, his body trembling with sheer hatred for her, he stepped up to her and rained a shower of blows to the top of her head.

"This is love, *ignoranta, stupida, ingrata....*" he hit her with each word, as if it were a blow to his own head, his body finally erupting at the sight of his mother's corpse.

Marie put her hands up to protect herself. He was crying and slapping at her hands. She grabbed hold of his wrists tightly, her strength overpowering him.

"Stop, Joey!" she cried. "Stop!"

He was unable to face her as she stood up, holding his wrists so tightly he felt handcuffed.

"She didn't even leave a note," he sobbed. "Nothing...."

His anger entirely subsided. There was only a terrible gaping grief.

They stood still for a moment, thinking about the enormity of his remark.

"She couldn't have, Joey," Marie said softly. "She just couldn't have."

And with that he put his arms around the stranger who was his sister and hugged her fiercely.

No words were spoken. It felt he was holding Annalise for a minute. But Annalise wasn't so thin and bony. Nor as stiff and unyielding in his arms. As if there were too many dark pockets of memory in her life that she couldn't expose. Because she had been transplanted onto unnatural and alien ground where she could never be herself.

And then it occurred to him in a rush of insight who it really was. That he hadn't missed his opportunity to touch her twice. That she was still in a way alive in his arms, thin and bony and still unyielding, like a proud tree torn from its roots and left to petrify on unnatural ground. It wasn't so much by words that he knew this as by sights and smells and feelings. Things that were ingrained in him deeper than words and language. Because he had been a branch of that tree, had been nurtured by its sap, and had broken off just in time not to be entirely poisoned.

That night the coroner called and informed him that preliminary results had shown that his mother had probably lost consciousness while walking on the tracks. Tests showed she had eaten so little in the past few days that she could easily have been prone to fainting spells. A report from the train engineer indicated that the shadow of the truss bridge had obscured his sight. He hadn't even seen her. The death would be pronounced an accident, with some unexplained circumstances. They could have the funeral at their convenience.

At that point he was too drunk to really care. He and Marie were in the upstairs kitchen well into their second bottle of wine. They had hardly spoken since his outburst. Only drinking to obliterate the pain.

In a heavily slurred voice he told Marie of the coroner's report. She merely nodded her head.

"It was all an accident," she shook her head. "Everything was an accident."

The wine was having a strange effect on her. She had put huge slices of cheese, along with half a loaf of bread, and assorted fruit in front of her and was eating and drinking ravenously, the food at times spilling out of her mouth. Her eyes were glazed. She smiled at him every so often, tenderly searching his face for forgiveness.

When she got tired of eating, she looked at him fondly. "Let's watch some television."

She walked over to the TV room unsteadily, opened the set and unthinkingly plopped herself onto Assunta's place at the end of the sofa. The screen came to life. He watched her silently. Her black dress. Her thin shrunken frame. Her lost eyes. And was confused for a moment.

Marie started switching channels indiscriminately with the remote-control. The screen went from program to program like a blur in front of his eyes. He started to feel sick to his stomach. He could feel himself being carried faster and faster into a dizzying nauseous circle. For a moment the screen stopped moving and he heard Marie say something.

"What did she mean, then, Joey?"

"Why don't you learn for yourself," he heard himself say impatiently.

"Can't you tell me?" she pleaded.

"No!"

"Please, Joey," she said, using the same tactic that had so often defeated him.

"You want to know what it means, uh? I'll show you what it means!"

And with that, as if by an instinct for self-preservation, he followed the direction of his scent to the empty chamber pot under the sofa. Marie stared at him with her mouth agape. His mind seemed to go blank. And with one violent heave he hurled the pot at the talking screen.

There was a shattering crash of glass. The sparks flashed and issued their last breath. Then there was smoke and an acrid smell of burnt wire and tubes. And finally silence.

After retching a few times later that night Joey managed to get to sleep.

He was on the familiar stretch of ice skating forward against the wind. Abruptly he braked as the wind changed. He saw a figure skating toward him on the icy reaches of the vast lake. There was a dazzling light reflecting off the ice that seemed to glow into a cloudless sky. Closer and closer the figure came. Joey froze when he saw it was dressed in a coal black uniform. And a black helmet. With a stick in its hands and its head bowed looking at the puck. He could hear the skate blades crunching into the ice and the pit-pats of the stick. His nose and ears were hard as stone, and it became difficult to breathe.

Then, unexpectedly, just as the figure came within yards of him and was about to lift his head, the ice started to crack open in front of him in a series of deafening reverberations. Joey was watching impassively. The figure desperately tried to maintain his footing. His stick flew out of his hands. His gloves clutched at the air. The ice broke into small chunks. The figure gave an animal scream of terror as he lost his balance.

In an instant he was sucked into the vast reaches of the inland ocean.

Before the funeral they had the widow Angeline help them write a cablegram to their aunt Pia in Novilara. Joey had suggested calling her, but there had never been a phone number as far as they could remember. They had included their number in case their aunt could make it to the funeral in time. An offer to pay her air fare had also been mentioned.

But Pia didn't call until after the funeral. Marie gave Joey the phone since he could speak better Italian. She went downstairs to listen in on the basement line. The voice was thin and distraught, crackling over the Atlantic from another world. Marie was immediately struck by the familiar ring to the accent and idiom. No-one from the West End had ever come from anywhere close to her mother's village in Marche.

Pia spoke quickly, trying to explain how she had received their news late because she lived on a farm a little way from the village. The cablegram had gone to Pesaro first, since the village didn't have a post office. She hadn't known what to do until a city friend told her to phone to America. But she hardly used the phone in the first place, she said by way of apology. She was afraid to phone so long a distance. Was Assunta really dead?

"*Sí,*" Joey said.

Pia went off the phone for a moment. She was talking to someone in the background. Marie could hear two women sobbing. When Pia came back she could scarcely talk. Joey tried to explain how it happened. It was very difficult for him to get the words out, but he managed to convey that it was an accident. Pia took it to mean her sister had died in a train accident. Joey left it at that. She kept sobbing, *povero Giuseppino, il tuo papà e la tua Mamma, c'è nesunno adesso*—there's no-one now—as if Joey were a child. It was the hand of God. And Assunta had so much wanted to come back to visit. She hadn't seen her in over 30 years. From that day in the train station in Pesaro when she had left with a suitcase and her trousseau trunk to go across the ocean to America.

"*Vieni in Italia,*" Pia said imploringly. "Come and live here, Giuseppe, for I know you like my own son. Assunta told me so many things about you. All she wrote to me about was you and Maria. I will take care of you. My roof is yours until you are married. Here, here, say hello to your sister, Marisa."

The shy timid voice of a young girl came on the line. It was a clear resonant voice that seemed to obliterate the ocean that separated them.

"*Ciao,* Giuseppe," Marisa said. "*Zia* Assunta was like a mother to me. She used to send me gifts and letters. I'm so sorry for you. Such a terrible accident. We all share your grief. You must come to Italia for my wedding in the summer, no."

For some reason Marie couldn't help sobbing at the sound of that voice. It was as if she could speak Italian.

"Is that you, Maria?" her cousin said. "*Ciao,* Maria. You must come to the wedding. Please. Maybe we can change our grief into happiness. I want to meet you and your little boy."

Marie made an attempt to say a few words, but her voice deserted her. She was overcome by an indescribable feeling of loss.

Pia wouldn't hang up until Marie and Joey convinced her that they'd seriously think about visiting them for the wedding. They'd have to keep in touch from now on.

The funeral was a quiet affair. This time there was no wailing at the bedside. Instead the Black Madonnas appeared in church together, sitting in the pew behind Marie and Joey. They were like a heavy black shroud mumbling their prayers in Italian in a continuous drone. Throughout the Mass Marie felt their eyes on her neck, burrowing into her.

She felt it was such a short step from the black dress to the black-draped casket in the aisle of the church.

Her eyes were fixed on the casket during the whole service. At the funeral home she had stared just as intently at her mother's shrunken death mask. Marie saw her own end sketched in the wrinkled and closed eyes—in the grey hair and the toothless mouth. She saw that her mother was nothing now, and that that nothing had been passed on to her in a place just under her heart where it was ticking with every beat, waiting to explode.

It was so certain she could almost taste her own end. The charred flesh. The smoke.

The certitude had caused such an overpowering fear that everything around her seemed to slip away into insignificance. Her heartbeat picked up. She could hear it reverberating in her head like a kettle drum. She had to close her eyes in the dimly lit parlour because the light was too glaring.

When it passed she burst into tears. Only a dizzy emptiness remained inside her.

After giving a short homily over the casket Father Sarlo, in an unexpected move, spoke personally about Assunta. His eyes glistened and his words rang with feeling and conviction in the empty church. He seemed to have to summon all his strength to speak.

He told of how he had come to know Assunta much more in the final months of her life. Of how she had opened her heart to him. She had trusted him. They had grown old together in the neighbourhood. They had eaten the Lord's meal together for a long time.

"She was a simple woman," he said, directing his eyes toward the living. "She came to this country from a small village. She was a peasant like you and me. It was difficult for her to leave her village. She was bewildered and very afraid. But she came nevertheless. God had destined her to marry someone in a new country, she said. Her parents were ashamed of her. She was well past the marriageable age. But they needed her to work on the farm. There was no dowry for her except a trousseau trunk. She knew this offer of marriage was her last chance. If there was one thing she wanted in all the world, she said, it was to have children. To make her life worthwhile, she said. She would have crossed all the oceans in the world for that. Her life had been filled with poverty and hunger. She lived on a small farm where the stable was part of the house. Where during bad years they ate *polenta* for months at a time. Nothing they had was theirs. She only wanted to be loved, she said.

"But I knew Assunta Barone before she told me these things. My mother was like Assunta Barone—and the mothers of many of my friends in our village in Calabria. And you know Assunta Barone, you older women who came to this country like her. Who were set in your ways. Who had the old country in your blood and nothing could wash it away. For Assunta it was harder than most. She couldn't even learn the language here. She watched so much TV to learn, she said, that the pictures spoke without the words.

"During the last months she told me often that she had failed her children. I tried to convince her that she hadn't failed anyone. That it was a different country with different people. She said that once she left the old country the only things she knew in life were to be a wife and mother.

"I say that she, with less than enough, has given all she had. May she rest in peace."

Immediately afterward Marie had turned around to look at the old women. Their eyes were downcast as their lips moved in prayer. They seemed not to have heard a thing.

The old priest's words, along with Pia's phone call, had left Marie deeply unsettled. She had the whole day to herself after the phone call. Joey had gone to Annalise's studio to do some work in order to keep his mind occupied and would be back later in the evening. While thinking of her mother she had a sinking fear that something had happened to Michael, that somehow she would be punished through her son.

"He's all right," Richard told her when she called. "I've just made him dinner and I'm beating the pants off him in Scrabble. How are things there?"

She told him about the funeral and the call from Italy. It

gave her such a feeling of relief to know that her home was intact, that she had somewhere to go where she was cared for and where she could care for someone. Her parents' house felt like an abandoned sinking ship. Its emptiness and silence were like screams of agony in her ears. It made her wonder if Joey had jumped off in time.

"It was so strange to discover these people knew so much about me. They even invited me over for a wedding this summer. Marisa, my cousin, is getting married."

"Why don't you go," Richard said. "You'll have the summer off. It'll be good for you after all these funerals."

"No, I couldn't."

"Sure, it could be just the thing."

She thought for a minute. "No, it's impossible, Richard. I couldn't do it."

"Why?"

"Italy is...it's just too far away, for one. And what about you and Michael?"

"You could take Michael, or leave him here with me if you wanted."

"What about you?"

In his pedantic tone he said, "Italy is something you have to come to terms with on your own, Marie. I'll just be in your way." And then with much spirit: "Besides, I'm definitely going to finish my book this summer."

"Let me speak to Michael," she said quickly.

But the suggestion wouldn't soon leave her. She had had enough of death. A wedding would perhaps set things in order again. It could possibly be the large Italian wedding she had never had herself. She could take Michael and let them see that Assunta's side of the tree hadn't completely withered. She could go back for her mother—make the return journey that Assunta had always wanted to make.

Marie wandered through the large empty house, momentarily excited by the possibility of going to visit her parents' homeland. To see first-hand where they had come from.

But the doomed house soon brought her back to the inescapable facts. The smashed TV set was a hideous reminder of the farces that had been played out in that room. In the stillness Marie could hear Assunta's voice asking them again and again what the actors were saying. Then the inevitable flare-up when she or Joey got fed up with the repeated interruptions. But why don't you learn the language? They'd raise their voices to her. Why don't you learn for yourself?

As she passed the front door she heard her mother yelling for her to come in for dinner, her voice ringing through the neighbourhood. Mar-yee-ya. Maaar-reee-yaaaaa. The name grating on her ears so much that she made sure it was Marie to everyone else.

In her old room she remembered the days of solitary confinement during high school. The endless books. The nights when all she did was homework until bedtime. The primping and preening in front of the mirror. To make herself different. To prepare herself for when she'd finally leave this island of foreignness and reach her true home.

Going downstairs again, she saw that she couldn't leave out her parents' bedroom any longer.

She opened the door slowly, half expecting to see them laid out on the bed, bordered by flowers. It was dark and stuffy inside. She noticed the time had passed quickly. Opening the windows, she saw the deserted street. The widow Angeline's house boarded up. The few old houses beyond the block still standing.

The room hadn't changed since her mother had cleared it after Adamo's funeral. Except for the change of dresser and headboard of the bed it was actually still the room of her childhood.

Almost in a daze Marie began looking for the key to the Hope Chest. It felt as if she were a child again, trying to find out how much her mother cared for her. Her value hidden in that old trunk.

After she searched long enough she took away the piles of

Grand Hotel from the top of the trunk. Marie opened one of them to see what her mother had found so fascinating in the magazines.

From the photographs she could see they hadn't changed much since she had looked at them as a girl. They were still the same serial depictions of love stories, with the dialogue set in comic-book fashion above the heads of the characters. As she leafed through a few of them she noticed that all the stories had well-groomed and handsome young men hopelessly in love with beautiful and fashionable young ladies, going through a series of difficulties before finding their right partners. Sometimes the love plots were set in a hospital, sometimes in a villa, but most often in a modern dazzling city where everyone drove the new Alfa Romeo or the latest Fiat. They were like endless soap operas, with people being shot at or suffering from unrequited love. But no matter what the difficulty, the characters always cut the *bella figura* of high Italian drama.

She recalled Father Sarlo's words: the pictures spoke without the words.

Taking away the cotton coverlet, she looked at the exposed chest for a minute. It was older and less sturdy than she remembered it. Its brown paint had peeled in places, leaving the grains of wood exposed like protuberant ribs. As if it too hadn't received enough nourishment over the years. The wood had become desiccated, and it sagged on top where the magazines had rested.

There was no need to fear breaking the top open now, she thought, as she went to the cantina to get the crowbar.

She noticed Adamo's mason's tools lying neatly on the workbench. The wine bottles almost all empty. The wine press and barrels in the corner. Maybe Joey could send her some wine every autumn. The potent stuff seemed to unleash a dark wild animal in her.

Back in the bedroom she sat on her haunches before the trunk and paused for a moment. This was it, she thought.

After all those fruitless years of searching. Yet it seemed to mean very little now. She had lost interest long ago. She had learned to live without her mother's Hope Chest.

Casually she reached over to see how securely the lid was locked.

To her utter surprise it moved.

She stayed still for a minute, thinking. She could hear the extra timepiece underneath her heart ticking.

Checking the locking mechanism, however, she shook her head and let out a sigh.

"*Stupida!*" she said out loud to herself.

There was no telling when it was unlocked. The mechanism looked rusted and unused, but it could have been unlocked only a few years ago—well past the time she had stopped looking. It was just that she hadn't conceived of it ever being left unlocked. She couldn't remember the last time she had checked, but it had to be before she was ten years old when her mother first started to tell her about the chest.

The lid opened easily. A reeking odour of moth balls and unaired clothing stung her nostrils. A yellowed sheet covered the contents like a shroud. By feel Marie could tell it was extremely old. She recalled Assunta saying that some of the contents went back for generations.

There was an assortment of bed linen and clothes immediately underneath. Pillow cases with ornate embroidery. A few towels. Some very simple cotton dresses. Common-sense underclothes of various patterns and fabrics. These seemed to have been mended recently. Underneath these was a simple black mourning dress of coarse black cotton with a kerchief and stockings. Marie noticed that as she dug deeper the contents appeared to be older, as if she were unearthing various layers of a person's life.

Without thought she draped the black dress over herself. It seemed to be the right size. Quickly she removed her jeans and shirt and tried it on. It smelled like an old book. Going in front of the mirror, she looked at her thin spectral frame.

She wasn't surprised that it fit like a glove. The dark patches under her eyes and her resigned ascetic expression seemed to suit the dress exactly.

Close to the bottom of the trunk were a couple of shoeboxes. She removed one and found what amounted to a shrine inside. There was a leather-bound frame that opened up into three pictures with a little stand underneath. One picture was of a sweet-looking young girl with her arms crossed over her heart looking angelically toward the sky. There were lilies in one hand and an aureole over her head. A church was in the far background. At the bottom was the name, S. Maria Goretti. On the opposite side was a photograph of an old white-haired peasant woman, solid and self-possessed, with a black polka dot kerchief, smiling serenely into the distance. The name underneath was Assunta Goretti. The middle photograph was of a casket underneath an altar in a church. The sides of the ornately made casket were of glass and the body of a young girl rested inside. She was wearing a full-length dress of glossy silk decorated with white lilies, and there was a crown on top of her long black hair. Her young virginal face was so composed that Marie thought she was only sleeping.

There was also an assortment of milk-white candles, a small font for holy water and various other religious items, such as two small statues of the Virgin, scapular medals and rosaries. The candles appeared to have been recently used.

Marie pictured her mother opening the case and lighting the candles underneath in the dark of her room.

But the image only made her more curious. She placed the picture-stand on the dresser and arranged the candles in front. Then she positioned the holy-water font and the two statues of the Virgin. She found some matches in the kitchen and lighted the candles. Shutting off the light she sat on the edge of the bed and looked into the mirror. Her face appeared just above the flames. The candles were reflected onto the bed behind her.

For a minute she thought of praying. She wondered who the people in the pictures were. Her mother had never mentioned them. She wondered what kind of people would keep the body of a girl under an altar. Whether it was the actual corpse. Or just a statue. The hair looked real.

She lost track of time as she sat transfixed in front of the shrine. Every so often she caught her own expression in the mirror. It was slightly perplexed. Slightly awed. It might have been one of her most complex mathematical problems she was facing.

Sometime later she felt her mother's presence in the room. She seemed to be lying on the bed behind her, the flowers bordering her body like icing on a cake. Marie stared harder into the mirror, trying to make out the expression on her mother's face. But she was too far away. She had to peer closer. The face came closer. It was hard like a statue. She saw the thin curve of the mouth. The sharp angular features. The deep-set eyes.

"Mamma, I'm sorry," she said out loud.

She waited patiently. Any answer, even no answer, would be all right. She felt her mind unloosen, clear itself of all cleverness and expectation. Slowly it extinguished itself and there was darkness.

The statued hardness of her mother's face softened. Colour was restored to the bony cheeks. The face twitched with life. The corners of her mouth slowly turned upward.

But the effort seemed to have exhausted Marie. She felt extremely faint. She remembered the only food she had eaten in days was yesterday's snack. The weight of her head was too much to hold up. Slowly she fell back onto the bed and closed her eyes.

Sometime later the overhead light abruptly awakened her. She didn't know where she was.

"Marie, what're you doing?"

Joey was standing at the door. His voice was thin and fearful. He looked startled, as he noticed the shrine and the opened Hope Chest.

"What's this?" he said.

"Shut the light," she said. It hurt her eyes.

He did as he was told.

"Let me be for a minute, Joey," she went on, as casually as she could. "I was only sleeping for a moment. Go on. I'll be out in a minute."

When she got her bearings she got up and blew out the candles. She put the shrine back in the shoebox and turned the light on. She was afraid to look at herself in the mirror.

Closing the trunk she saw she had forgotten the other shoebox. To her great delight it was full of old photographs of Assunta and her family in the old country.

Marie took the box and brought it to the kitchen to show Joey.

Her brother appraised her quizzically.

"Where did you get that dress?" he said.

"In the Hope Chest."

"What was going on in there?"

"I just found some things in the trunk. A religious shrine."

"You scared me," he said.

"Sorry, I only got tired and fell asleep for a while."

"You know, with that dress on and lying on the bed, I thought..."

"Look what else I found," she said abruptly, dumping the photographs on the table.

They went through them without further word, as if starved for information on their mother. They were like still-lifes of Assunta's past. There were photos of Assunta playing in vineyards and under fig trees. Of Assunta's father separately, with a large bushy moustache and in his best dark suit, in a Napoleonic pose. Of Assunta's mother, thin and wasted, alone in a cave-like mediaeval kitchen. Of Assunta as a child squatting on the dirt floor of what seemed like a shed. Of Assunta growing up. Her first communion. Her first pair of good shoes. Of her and Pia doing their chores. Of weddings to which the family had been invited. Of the black-bordered commemorations of dead relatives.

Through the pictures Marie got a good sense of the land her mother came from. It was hilly, with every piece of available land used for cultivation. A few pictures showed men ploughing fields that were strewn with rocks. The village itself rested on top of a hill. It seemed to have been some sort of fortress at one time. There was a picture of Assunta, at about nine or ten, in a pinafore, walking with Pia down a winding road, with part of a large crenellated wall and gate behind them.

As she was going through the photos of her grandparents and various relatives she saw the kind of people she came from. Hardy men with grizzly sun-bleached faces and high cheekbones. Stout and black-draped women hunched and hardened by toil. People of the earth. Peasants who worked all their lives trying to eke an existence from the soil. It was hard to believe their blood flowed through her veins.

It seemed the only son in her mother's family had died young and there were only two girls to help out with the farm.

"Why do you think Ma never showed us these?" Joey asked her, captivated by the photographs.

"I don't know," she said pensively. "I remember as a girl I used to think she was trying to hide some fantastic secret from us. A scandal maybe. Like she was the illegitimate daughter of a grand duke sent to America to safeguard a reputation. So I could be proud of being her daughter."

Looking over more pictures Marie went on: "It seems, though, that what Father Sarlo said is true."

"You were always asking why she force-fed us," Joey said, handing her a picture. "Look at this."

It showed a scrawny sickly Assunta at fourteen or so, with Pia and their mother, seated at the kitchen table. They were all wearing shabby nondescript dresses. There was an iron pot in the middle of the table, with empty plates for four. The mother, with her back to the camera, was ladling out what appeared to be a thin soup. Assunta and the younger Pia had spoons in their hands and were facing the camera with long sad countenances. Marie couldn't tell why the father would record such a moment, unless it was of a happy occasion. In the background, a little way from the fireplace where the iron pot was obviously hung, a door was open and Marie could clearly make out the side of an animal.

Marie could only shake her head.

"Do you want any of these?" she asked Joey. "I'd like to keep the rest."

"Maybe a few of Mamma. And grandfather and grandmother. What else is in the trunk?"

"It's just a simple trousseau trunk with bed linen and some other necessities."

"Are you going to keep it? It's yours, you know." He was looking intently at her.

"Did you know it was opened?"

He shook his head.

She thought for a moment, noticing for the first time a framed painting resting on the floor behind him.

"I was thinking of taking it to Italy to give to Marisa as a wedding gift," she said in a resigned tone. "I don't deserve it and she can probably make better use of it than I can."

"Then you're going?" he said, excited for her.

She nodded. "I think I'll be able to make it. What about you?"

"I can't, really. There's the house still. Someone should be here. I still have to find a new place. Someday I'll go over, though, and see for myself.

Marie reached over and put her hand on his shoulder.

"What're you going to do with all their stuff?"

"I don't know about the personal stuff. But the rest—the furniture, wine press, and things like that—I'll keep or sell."

He smiled. She smiled softly back at him.

"Is that Annalise's work?" she indicated the painting behind him.

It showed the side view of a hockey player with a close resemblance to Joey skating all alone over a large expanse of ice in the outdoors. The skater was midway between the glassy-smooth ice and the reddish sky, his eyes intent upon a point in the horizon, his face dark and fervent. The sun was setting in a cloudless sky and casting a long shadow on the ice.

Joey laughed, "Annalise thinks she's transferred all the passion I've had for hockey onto her. Notice the fierce expression on his face."

Joey's spontaneous laugh was so unexpected that she was compelled to look closer at him. And as she saw his hard wide jaw and thick potent eyebrows it occurred to her how much more real he was to her than ever before. That somehow the way he felt life was the measure of his reality.

"I'm very happy for you, Joey," she said.

He shook his head. "I can't believe what I did to the TV set."

"You can buy another one."

His expression changed abruptly. He looked sorrowfully into her eyes.

"I have to tell you this, Marie. I told Ma about selling the house. I couldn't help it."

He told her about what happened that day with Assunta and Annalise in the kitchen. He had lost his temper. She had treated him as a kid once too often.

"I tried my best," he put his head down on the table.

Marie looked tenderly at her brother.

"It's all right, Joey," she said, her voice full of forgiveness. "It's all right."

She put her hand on his head and stroked it fondly.

On the table she looked into the hungry eyes of her mother and smiled.

13

Joey buttered the brick slowly, making sure the edges received equal amounts of mortar. Then he placed it in the last slot of the line, trimmed the excess mortar, and furrowed the joints.

He was close to the apex of the pyramid. It was coming out just as he had planned. He had read up about it and had made a master plan, using some drafting equipment from high school. The base was square and the four triangular sides faced the points of the compass, sloping at an angle of 50 degrees to the ground so that they'd meet at the apex.

The base of the pyramid took up almost the complete width of the garden. Around it, the rest of the area was littered with materials. Pieces of broken brick. Bags of cement and lime. A crate of bricks. A wheelbarrow with wet mortar.

He was draped along one side of the structure that was as high as the roof of the garage.

When Annalise first saw it she laughed and called it an example of Minimal Art.

"It's elemental," she said, grinning at him. "It has inertia. And it's ambiguous."

Actually she had given him the idea once when she talked of this man who had built a fence running through the width of the state of California—and then had it dismantled as soon as it was finished. She had been disparaging. It had taken much money and corporate management to build. But here it was only him using his father's tools in his back garden.

"It's minimal talent, more likely," he said, laughing with her.

It was the end of August and his last day in the house. Everything that he hadn't sold was packed and ready to go. Except his parents' personal stuff. Donny and Annalise would help him move to his new apartment in the East End.

He had been working on the pyramid for weeks. Marie had flown to Italy at the beginning of the month. He had gone down to Toronto with Annalise to see her off. At the airport in front of the last gate Marie was very apprehensive. She was dressed in the black dress she had found in the trunk.

"It'll be a strange trip," she said, looking slightly bewildered. "I hope they'll be there."

Pia and Marisa and her fiancé were to drive across Italy to Rome to pick her up at the airport.

Joey hugged his sister. Wished her a good trip.

"I'll tell you everything when I come back, Joey," she whispered in his ear.

Richard appeared stiff. He made a joke about her dress to ease the tension. Michael asked her when she was coming back. The people going through the gate looked very Italian and his sister didn't look out of place.

Later, he and Annalise went to see as many art galleries as they could. They stayed at Marie's place. Annalise slept in the nursery with Michael.

Joey found that he derived immense satisfaction from laying bricks. The tools felt good in his hands. Although he was making something that wouldn't last, it nevertheless would be hard to tear down.

Annalise said she would be bringing her camera to take photographs of the pyramid.

"For posterity?" he said.

"For you," she said.

Slowly he crept down the side of the structure to get the last handful of bricks. It was twilight and there was a clear sky. When he went back up he could see the sun setting just behind the silhouette of the steel plant. Quickly he put the few remaining bricks in place with the trowel.

Then he split the last brick in half and placed it on the very top.